A STUDY IN DETAIL

A STUDY IN DETAIL

MICHAEL GUILLEBEAU

FIVE STAR

A part of Gale, Cengage Learning

GALE
CENGAGE Learning·

Farmington Hills, Mich • San Francisco • New York • Waterville, Maine
Meriden, Conn • Mason, Ohio • Chicago

LIBRARY OF CONGRESS CATALOGING-IN-PUBLICATION DATA

Guillebeau, Michael.
    A study in detail / Michael Guillebeau. — First edition.
        pages ; cm
        ISBN 978-1-4328-2985-8 (hardcover) — ISBN 1-4328-2985-8
    (hardcover) — ISBN 978-1-4328-2978-0 (ebook) — ISBN 1-4328-
    2978-5 (ebook)
        1. Married people—Fiction. 2. Missing persons—Investiga-
    tion—Fiction. I. Title.
    PS3607.U4853S78 2015
    813'.6—dc23   2014038267

First Edition. First Printing: February 2015
Find us on Facebook– https://www.facebook.com/FiveStarCengage
Visit our website– http://www.gale.cengage.com/fivestar/
Contact Five Star™ Publishing at FiveStar@cengage.com

DEDICATION

I came of age in the 1960s, which doesn't necessarily mean what you think. The first half of the sixties was dominated by the straight-shooting good guys: the Matt Dillons and Andy Griffiths who just wanted to live simple, happy lives and take care of things. Later in the decade, that intellectual bud of simple goodness flowered into the passionate attitudes of questioning-everything and taking-care-of-the-whole-universe that we usually associate with the time.

Both halves of that single coin shaped me then and shape me now as I struggle to live up to the Andy Griffiths and the Martin Luther Kings and Joan Baezs running around in my head. This book is largely driven by those pillars of my life.

So this book is dedicated to all of the good boys and good girls of the 1960s, struggling still to be good and not just to be what they're told to be. And especially to one girl who is still the best thing this poor struggling boy has ever seen.

ACKNOWLEDGMENTS

I've got to first thank two amazing young writers whom you've never heard of but someday will: Jeremy Bronaugh and Cheryl Rydbom. There is as much of them in this book as there is of me. Guys, I cannot thank you enough.

Thanks to Randy Bachmeyer and Jolie Guillebeau for both technical and literary help.

And, as always, thanks to the best first reader any writer ever had: Pat Leary Guillebeau.

After a book is written, it's all just lonely words on a page until someone believes in it. First, Janet Hutchinson and her fine folks at *Ellery Queen's Mystery Magazine* believed in *Study* enough to publish the beginning as a short story. Then the magic folks at Five Star Mysteries believed in it, too. Deni Dietz and Gordon Aalborg worked long and hard to make *A Study in Detail* a better book and me a better writer. Thanks, guys.

And the most important step is the last: you the reader. Thank you for reading *A Study in Detail*. I hope you enjoy it, and I hope you drop me a line at michaelguillebeau@gmail.com to tell me what you think, good or bad. I am profoundly grateful that you have given me and Paul and Rue a piece of your busy lives.

CHAPTER 1

She loved us both, and that was a big part of what made me love her. Other people didn't understand: they just saw me alone at parties where she was supposed to be, apologizing again because Marta was caught up in a painting and couldn't be bothered. Like most vicious things, their comments were always camouflaged as sympathy: "Too bad she doesn't see what this does to you," or "All this, and nobody wants to buy her paintings." But I just smiled and imagined her home at her easel, humming away while she worked on something new rather than enduring small conversations with small minds and trying to keep a small smile on her face.

Her paintings mattered to her, and her causes mattered to her, and I mattered to her and not much else mattered in her world. I figured that anyone who had that kind of intensity had plenty for me. And I was right. At least, until lately.

When I woke up she was already out on her bike doing her penance or meditation or whatever it was. A couple of years ago, she had started running errands around Portland on an old beach cruiser and found out she thought best and felt most alive on her bike. After a lot of prodding from me, she graduated to a red Felt FW25, light as the wind and twice as fast. She would fly along a ten mile loop around the lake all day, stopping for coffee and food at a little convenience store where the owner from the tiny African country of Leongo always asked about her mileage. Flying along on her own, working out details in her head of something she was working on, or maybe on details of something else in her life that wasn't working.

When they worked, the rides were magic for her, ideas for paintings spinning as fast and smooth as her pedals. But her paintings weren't selling, and she took it personally. The world was rejecting her children and she didn't know what to do about it. So the bike miles were turning into miles looking for blame, and the blame was coming home more and more to me. Sometimes, if the world kicks you, you kick your dog. If you don't have a dog, you kick your spouse.

Counterproductive, I know, but we all do it.

I told her one day, "Make a change; any change."

She said, "I want a new life."

After a long pause where neither one of us said anything, she said she didn't know what that meant or why. I told her to find a way, just find a way. She suffered for her children; I suffered for her. We were all suffering, and we were all tired of it.

I went for a run and came back into the kitchen to get a cup of coffee and see if she was back. In my empty cup was a note: "Enjoy your new baby and your new life." Cryptic, but typical Marta.

She had locked me out of the studio for the last week, didn't want me to see something until it was done. She sometimes did that, and then, when it was done, she couldn't bear to see my reaction first hand. So I knew where she was: out on her bike, flying around and around the ten mile lake loop until she was sure I was awake and had seen her new baby.

I took my coffee and went up the stairs to the third-floor studio we'd made by gutting the whole floor into one open room with big windows on every side and a couple of skylights in the roof. There was a big, bright new painting in the middle, waiting. It was a portrait of me, full-length. I had to laugh: she had painted me in electric blue workman's overalls, with tools coming out of every pocket. I got it. Once we had gotten into a terrible fight: one in a series of recurring fights that we seemed to have over and over with no way out. At the time, she was ranting about something, anything, it never seemed to matter what as long as she had something to rant about. I was trying to come up with solutions. Every solution I came up with just made her madder until she screamed, "Paul, the Practical Man. Paul, the Fixer." Somehow, that caught her, and she started giggling and got her own joke. "That's just who you are," she said. "You live in the real world; I have to live in my own imagination. That's who you are. Paul, the Practical Man." The fight was over, it never came back, and that was her nickname for me from then on.

So there I was that morning, Paul the Sweaty Runner with a Cup of Coffee in His Hand admiring Paul the Practical Man. She had found a new technique. Somehow, Paul the Practical Man seemed to float a couple of feet out from the rest of the painting, glowing. I was trying to figure out how she had done that, when I noticed the title painted in a scroll across the bottom: "For Paul, Who Understands." I looked at my face in the painting. It had a big smile, bigger than any I'd ever smiled, but it also had a tear. That was one of Marta's trademarks: contradiction. Every painting had to have two meanings, or it never made it out of her studio.

I stepped closer. The background appeared dark from fifteen feet away, but up close I could see that there was much more. There was a cabin where we had spent our first weekend together. The beach where we spent our honeymoon. Or where I spent it; she spent it in a back room, lost on a watercolor that she'd got an idea for on the flight down. Just had to finish it, just had to or the idea would run away. There was more: there I was with a sledgehammer, smashing our first kitchen table. I had spent hours putting the damned thing together with the damned Ikea directions, and she burst into tears and said, "I hate it, I just hate it, I'm sorry, but I just hate it." So I took a sledge that I was using to remodel the upstairs and smashed the thing that I hated building and she hated looking at. Didn't solve the problem, of course, but it sure felt good.

The painting had all of our history somewhere in the background, and that was Marta's other trademark, and the one that killed her commercial appeal: she worked in careful layers, letting each layer dry so the backgrounds of her paintings had fantastic details. If you would spend an hour with anything of hers, you would spend two, and then three and more until you could follow the whole fantastic story she told with tiny brush strokes in giant paintings. But, of course, if you just spent thirty seconds in a gallery, you walked away unimpressed with "that red thing" or "that blue thing."

I went downstairs to call the shop and tell them I'd be late. This one would take all morning. I made myself a Nutella sandwich to take upstairs and heard someone at the door.

I thought it was Marta, forgetting her keys again and sure I'd be there to let her in. I was going to tell her to get back on her bike for the rest of the morning while I finished adopting the new baby, but I saw Larry through the glass. Larry was our family lawyer and the owner of the gallery where Marta's work usually opened, and was the closest thing to an agent that Marta had.

"Come on in, Larry," I said. "You missed Marta. She's out on her bike again and she may be gone a long, long time."

Larry stood there with his mouth open like I'd said something strange, but I didn't know what. Larry knew about Marta and her bike and didn't like it. Larry was all business and dealt with everything in the now. Marta would disappear on her bike for hours and refuse to be interrupted by carrying a cell phone.

Larry closed his mouth.

"Yeah, I know." He pushed past me into the house. "Come on in and sit down, Paul. We need to talk.

"The police just left the gallery. They found Marta's bike on the bridge. It's been run over, and there's no sign of Marta. There's blood on the rail, too, but at this point, they're not sure if it's hers." He took a breath. "I'm sorry. I didn't know any way to tell you but to just tell you. I didn't want you to hear it from the police. Or the radio."

I started to say something but he held up his hands.

"Maybe she's OK, Paul. The police are searching the area, and we can get down there and help. Maybe she's sitting in somebody's house right now, waiting for you."

"Maybe," I said, starting to plan what to do. I knew the bridge, and it was a high one, so high that there was usually a suicide from it every couple of years. This is a pretty bike-friendly area, but this particular bridge was a battleground between bikers and traffic. There was a footbridge half a mile away that bikers could use, if they would walk their bikes across. Bikers asserted their right to the bridge; some drivers, particularly some truckers, went out of their way to intimidate the bikers. There had been incidents in the last couple of years, one conviction of a driver, and one death from a hit-and-run that nobody saw.

"I know the river as well as anybody around here. I'm going to get my river clothes on and take a kayak down there," I said.

Larry stopped me. "There's something we need to talk about first, Paul."

He took a breath. "You remember Jonathon Crowley? Worked in acrylics, did little pieces with odd shapes?"

I thought about it and realized where he was going. "No, Larry, that's not what happened."

Larry hesitated. "Probably not. But it's something you need

to consider. Nobody loved their paintings more than Marta loved hers. She didn't care that much about the money or fame herself, but it tore her up that her paintings didn't find the homes she thought they deserved. Every time I had to move one of her paintings into storage, I knew I had a big fight coming, like I had just locked one of her kids in a closet and wasn't going to let him out.

"You know what happened with Crowley. Big success after he commit . . . died. Off that same bridge. Marta talked about it all the time, maybe he had done the right thing, that kind of talk. Another thing: you know how Marta likes to make a statement and how she loves that bike. This will get something done on that bridge, maybe bike lanes or barriers or something.

"I'm not saying she did anything overt. Maybe just a swerve before the sun came up." He looked at me and shrugged. "Maybe not. You know, I don't know why I brought it up. I'm sure she's OK."

"You don't know Marta," I said.

But we both knew that he knew Marta better than anyone but me.

CHAPTER 2

We'd left the front door open, and there was a man standing there: pale skin, white hair, a thin ghost in jeans and a brown sport coat. He was holding up a badge.

"Excuse me, sir," he said. "I'm Detective Martin Ahlstrom. Sounds like you've already been told what happened." He glared at Larry.

"Yeah, but not details," I said. "Any sign of her in the river? She's a good swimmer. She can make it to shore."

"The rescue squad's down there, sir. We've got men going to every house in every neighborhood downstream." He looked at Larry and me like he was examining a science project. "Sounded like you two were trying to get your stories straight when I walked in. Anything either one of you want to say?"

Larry shook his head.

"We're going to find her," I said.

"No," Ahlstrom stepped toward me. "We—the police—are going to find her. You and your pal are coming down to the station, separately, for questioning. I don't like what I overheard, and I want to hear more."

"I'm going to the river and find Marta," I said. "We'll talk later. You can talk to Marta, then, too."

"I'll ask her why she was on that bridge before dawn," he said, pushing his nose almost into mine. "Ask her why she wasn't on the walkway instead of playing in traffic."

I looked at him a slow second and realized he was trying to

15

make me lose my temper and say something stupid.

"The walkway's for pedestrians," I said. "The bridge is for vehicles, including bikes. You need to read the law, and you need to enforce it. What about the driver? What did he say?"

He looked back with a long emotionless stare. "No sign of him. Just a crunched up bike found in the middle of the road, and some blood on the rail that we're testing now." He paused and watched me for a reaction. "And I will enforce the laws. All of them."

"You should have traffic cameras there. Marta may be able to help identify the driver, when we find her. Someone needs to pay for what's happening to bikers on that bridge. If you people had done your job before, Marta would be standing here safe now."

Same dead-eyed stare. "We do our job, sir. Even if it means harassing truck drivers trying to earn an honest living while dodging big kids playing in the road."

"Enough of this crap. I'm getting my stuff and getting out on the river. Call me on my cell if you get anything. My wife needs me."

The detective started to say something, but Larry put his hand on his arm. "Detective, Mr. McClaron owns the kayak store just below the bridge. He knows the river better than anyone around. If Marta's in the river, he'll find her."

Detective Ahlstrom thought about that. "So you own the landing below the bridge where your wife disappeared? Boy, that's convenient. You weren't down there in the middle of the night by any chance?"

"What are you implying? That Mr. McClaron ran over his wife on the bridge with a kayak?" Larry was now slouching slightly with the little relaxed smile that showed he was slipping into his shark lawyer pose.

"No, just asking questions. At this point, I don't know if anybody ran over anybody else, if we've got an accident or a disappearance or what. While I'm asking questions, sir, may I ask what your involvement is in this?"

"I am Mr. McClaron's lawyer. Also his wife's."

Ahlstrom's eyes widened and it took him an effort to look bored.

"So you just happened to get here ahead of the police, talking to your client about a disappearance so fresh the police haven't even notified the next of kin?"

"Yeah. I was notified by Lieutenant . . ."

"Good to have connections, isn't it, sir?" Ahlstrom turned his back on Larry. "And you own a kayak shop a couple of hundred yards from where your wife disappeared?"

"This is crap," I said. "I'm going to the river. Marta can tell you for herself when I find her."

"Sir, don't leave. You and your attorney are coming down to the station. We've got men searching for your wife. We can talk while they work."

Larry's standard friendly-lawyer smile flickered a little bigger, like we were just standing around talking basketball.

"So you're arresting my client?"

"No sir. You're both coming voluntarily for questioning."

"Have you ever had a citizen's complaint filed against you, Detective? Ever caused the department to be sued for harassment on your behalf?"

Ahlstrom didn't say anything, but a smile flickered like a little boy caught stealing cookies and proud of it.

"Then get out of my client's way," said Larry. "He's got work to do."

Ahlstrom stood there for a moment. "Tell you what," he said. "I'll give you a choice. I know the river, too. I'll change clothes and meet you at the landing. You've got a two man kayak there, right? I'll go with you, and we can talk while we look."

"There's no way my client's spending the morning alone with you," said Larry.

"Then all three of us will spend the morning in an interview room."

I held up my hand. "Deal," I said. "Don't get in the way."

Larry started to say something, saw the look on my face and just shook his head. They left and I ran into the bedroom and pulled on waterproof pants and a Gore-Tex jacket. I'd get a kayak and a pack with food and water from the store while I was waiting on Ahlstrom.

CHAPTER 3

"That's kind of neat," said Ahlstrom. He was standing at the edge of the Willamette River by an orange kayak I was loading. He was holding up a standard two-blade paddle, testing grips. He was still wearing his suit pants with a blue windbreaker with "Police" on it.

He said, "They give you two blades on these instead of the one blade we had on canoe paddles when I was a kid." He paddled the air on one side, showing me his expertise. "I guess that's so you've got a backup in case one breaks."

I stared at him.

"You said you knew the river."

"Drive past it every day."

I bit my lip and took a deep breath and forced myself to slow down. Lot of help I was going to get from this guy.

"OK," I said. "I'll need your help out there. Here's what you do." I picked up my paddle and stood in front of him and showed him how to hold the paddle. He fumbled and I guided his hands to the same position as mine and I looked at him and saw the steel of beady little eyes measuring every word and gesture of mine, looking for a hesitation a microsecond too long or any contradiction from one story to the next. I felt like a lab rat wired up to a machine. I snapped back to why we were here.

"Never mind," I said. I took the paddle out of his hands and stowed it under the bungee cords along the side of the kayak. "I'll paddle."

"Yeah, makes sense," said Ahlstrom. "You're a big guy. You're what—thirty-five? Yeah, you do the work. Let the little old guy sit here and ask questions."

I pushed the kayak's nose into the water. "You get in the front."

"No, you get in the front. I don't like people looking at my backside."

My mouth got tight.

"Look, I told you not to get in the way. Marta's out there somewhere. Time matters. Get in or stay out."

He stood there watching.

"The person who knows how to paddle has to sit in the back," I said.

He grumbled and got in, almost tipping the kayak. I pushed the kayak in a little deeper, climbed in, and pushed us out into the river.

Ahlstrom started to pull his paddle free.

"I'll paddle," I said. "Leave that alone and keep quiet."

"I just want to pull my weight."

"Yeah, well, tell you what. I've got a paddle, you've got a gun. I'll paddle. You watch out for alligators."

He jerked around and looked at me, almost capsizing us.

"There are alligators out here?"

"All over the place. Keep your eyes open."

He opened his eyes wide in mock panic but I could see him smile to himself as he turned around.

"Alright," I said, pulling us out into the current. I drifted and looked up toward the bridge. "You seem to have plenty of boats and men around the bridge."

"Looking for evidence."

"Yeah, well, they can look for evidence. We're looking for Marta. You ever think of trying that, follow that 'serve and protect' motto a little bit instead of trying to trick people so you can collect another arrest."

"I guess I'm more like the collector type." He turned around and almost put us in the river again. He was smiling and friendly. "See, when I was young, just starting out . . ."

"For crying out loud, I didn't come out here to listen to your life story. Just keep your eye on the river and let me think."

He frowned and turned around.

I started paddling. "Your men have the bridge, so we're going downstream. I'm going to put us in the current, try to follow and catch up with Marta. You watch the right bank. Watch for anything: something disturbed on the bank, a houseboat she might have swum to."

Ahlstrom added. "A body floating along with a knife in her back and her husband's fingerprints on it, maybe a receipt for a plane ticket that helped her disappear . . ."

"For crying out loud!" I yelled and he turned around and grinned at me like the village idiot he was.

"Is that all you got?" he said. "You know, how a man curses tells you a lot about him. Supposedly, your wife is missing and you know nothing about it, a cop makes a shitty remark, and all you can say is, 'for crying out loud'?"

"My momma raised me with better manners than that."

"Aw, come on. Let me hear you say, 'Shut the hell up.' "

I tried. "Shut the h up."

Ahlstrom smiled. "See . . . got you pegged."

"Good for you. Now watch the shore. Find Marta. Just keep repeating that to yourself. Find Marta and take me off your suspect list."

He turned back to the front and said over his shoulder, "You're not a suspect. Just a guy I'm having a friendly chat with. I like friendly chats."

"You have a lot of friends?"

"None."

I scanned the river for anything unusual: people shouting on the bank, a little group of boats huddled around something, anything. There was nothing.

"Then stop chatting and let me think. I got up about seven; Marta was gone then. Don't know how much earlier she left, but let's assume she went off the bridge at seven just to have a place to start. So she's got about a three-hour head start. Marta can survive three hours in the river if she has to."

"What time did you go to bed?" he said.

"Eleven-thirty, maybe midnight."

"Didn't get up in the middle of the night anytime? Notice if she was around?"

"No." I was irritated and only half paying attention to him.

"Not even to pee?"

"No."

"See, now, I don't understand that. Me, I'm up at least once every night. Since I turned fifty, it's usually a couple of times. My doctor says I need to get checked out, but I'm not going to let some fat old man stick his finger . . ."

My attention drifted completely away from listening, and I felt like that's all we were doing out here: drifting. I suddenly realized what Ahlstrom was talking about and snapped at him.

"What is wrong with you? I did not come out here to discuss your prostate."

"Just saying."

"Well, don't. Hey, what's that?" I said.

"What?"

"Over there. Something red, by that piling. End of the dock with the Hobie cat tied up to it." I started to pick up the pace.

"Yeah, I see it. Was she wearing a red jacket when she left?"

"Maybe. She's got a couple of jackets, one red like that." I paddled furiously to get us lined up and headed for the random brush stroke of red on the dark gray water.

"You didn't notice what she was wearing this morning when you got up at eight?"

"Seven." I was breathing hard. "Thought I wasn't a suspect."

"You're not." Ahlstrom turned back with that idiot's grin. "For now."

CHAPTER 4

It was the right color and shape. The closer I got, the surer I was. I could see Marta's black hair, then an arm. There. The arm moved. She was alive, she needed me, and she needed me now. It was hard to keep a steady rhythm in my paddling and not just flail the water in a furious effort that would feel good but accomplish nothing.

"Did you hear me?" said Ahlstrom, still looking back at me. Same idiot grin waiting for me to respond. "Said you're not a suspect, for now."

I didn't even bother telling him to shut up and look forward. I was going to save Marta and I didn't need his help or care what he thought.

Ten yards away, I stopped paddling and we coasted in. Ahlstrom reached over the side.

He gave an aggravating little laugh. "Heh heh heh. Your wife always wear a trash bag when she's bike riding or disappearing or being killed by her husband?"

He held up the orange-red trash bag. The branch that looked like an arm, the chunk of black wood I thought was hair, drifted away in the current like the nothing they were. Ahlstrom dropped the trash bag back into the river. I backed the kayak out into the river and blinked my eyes until they were clear.

Twenty yards out, I stopped and paddled back and picked up the trash bag and threw it between my feet to throw out when we got back.

"Boy Scout," said Ahlstrom. "Knew you couldn't leave trash in your river."

"Don't you ever shut up?"

He bared his teeth again in an awkward attempt at a friendly grin. "You know, when I get off a case, I'm a real quiet guy. But get me on a case, and I can't stop talking. Just keep thinking out loud, say the obvious things that everybody else is thinking, wait for somebody to say something that agrees with me. You know, I really am good at my job."

"Surprised that somebody hasn't killed you. Or at least fired you."

"They would, if I wasn't good at catching killers. Nobody likes me, not even on the force. Even my mom used to call me, 'Martin the Martian.' Thought I was weird."

"Imagine that."

"Heh heh heh," he said. "You know, there was this one time . . ."

"Can you just shut the heck up?" I yelled.

"Probably not. Only people I get to really talk to are perps like you. Then I get to say anything I want, you can't do nothing about it. I—"

I grabbed the sides of the kayak and shook it furiously. Ahlstrom turned even paler and grabbed the kayak for support.

"Hey," he said.

"Look, we're not out here on a picnic and we sure aren't friends. Just one more word, and I'm putting you in the river and going on without you. You just have to solve a case, don't care whether Marta's alive or not. I have to save Marta."

Ahlstrom looked horrified. "That's assaulting an officer."

"No, but it will be." I shook the kayak again.

Ahlstrom pulled out a little notebook and hunched over it, scribbling furiously. But at least he was quiet.

I turned back into the channel and scanned the banks until I realized they were becoming blurry. I pulled my bandana off and wiped my eyes. The blurriness came back and I wiped them again. Gritted my teeth and told myself that tears wouldn't save Marta.

And I was going to save Marta. This awful event would be a turning point and a way forward for us.

Marta and I had been falling apart for months. There was a hole in her soul that she could not talk to me about. Every pointless, vicious fight ended with "you just don't understand" and I knew that Marta was an artist who felt things deeper than I did, and I knew how much she was hurt when the world didn't love her art, but I felt like there was something more. I spent hours alone on the river trying to figure out what could hurt her so much. She couldn't talk to me about it, and I kept coming back to one thing: the dissatisfaction in her life was me. The simple man who just wanted everything to be all right all the time. Paul the Practical Man.

But I was going to save her now. And after that, I was going to save us.

We stayed on the river until it was too dark to see. I pushed the kayak hard to get back and then watched Ahlstrom drive away from the dock in his unmarked Chevy Impala. Got in my old Suburban and cruised the river banks until even Portland coffee couldn't keep my eyes open and I went home to lie down for a couple of hours before I would meet Ahlstrom at dawn to go back on the river.

CHAPTER 5

I lay on our bed for an hour that felt like a week. The things I saw when I closed my eyes were worse than the darkness I saw when I opened them, so I got up and made a pot of coffee and put some Nutella on two slices of bread and carried the cup and the sandwich upstairs and sat in front of the painting.

Something was wrong. At first I thought the coffee or the Nutella or the bread was bad. I sniffed them and smelled nothing but the richness of coffee and chocolate. But there was still something in the air.

Cloves. Marta's studio was reeking with the sweet, earthy smell. Oil of cloves. Marta sometimes used a little to keep oil paint from drying out. I sniffed around the room and wound up back at the painting where the smell was strongest.

I ignored the figure of Paul the Practical Man and followed the story in the details in the background. It was our life, or at least the happy memories and none of the fights. Until you came to the end in the bottom right corner, which was just a bright orange splash. Sunrise. Sunset. Explosion. There was no way to tell which.

I stepped aside to pick up my sandwich and stopped with it halfway to my mouth. From this angle, one scene in the painting was glossy. Still wet, even a day later.

The cabin where we spent our first weekend was just a small detail, something no one but me would notice. The gravel road leading to the cabin was just a few swipes of grey paint. But there was a bridge before the cabin, and the bridge was missing. There was a gap where the bridge should be, a blue swatch where the water cut the road in two. It wasn't right.

I got a light, and a magnifier. There was another layer behind the road, and the paint on the top layer was still wet. I picked up a can of turpentine and a rag and started carefully removing paint, as fast as I could without disturbing the lower layer. There was writing. After a few minutes, I could read it.

"If you come for me, they will hurt my children."

I stood there for a long time, watching the world spin around and fall out from under my feet. Marta was alive and I was alone. In that moment, my future changed from a heroic rescue to a life of pretense and loneliness. Marta had left me. But Marta was alive, somewhere.

I knew then that I wouldn't find Marta, and I knew that she was right about what she said. We treat tragedy with admiration, failure with contempt. The paintings of a dead artist would get attention and find homes. The paintings of an artist who had faked her death, and been caught, would be laughed at. Marta's palette was still wet. I picked it up, disguised the writing, and quickly painted the road back, adding the bridge. I opened the windows to let the room air out.

For the sake of Marta's children, I searched the river and tolerated Ahlstrom for a week. For Marta's children, I traveled and lectured on her work, and her paintings got the attention they deserved. There is an obligation and a price in loving someone, and an obligation and a price in loving what they love. For the sake of Marta's children, I would not search for Marta.

And did not.

Publicly.

CHAPTER 6

I was out on the river, drifting and alone. An early spring morning, a rare sunny day in Portland six months after Marta's disappearance.

Most mornings, I kayaked on the Willamette River until the sun came up and the river filled me with calmness and comfort but today she was just cold and silent and withdrawn from me. It should have been a beautiful soul-warming morning. But my mind, restless and unfocused, was back in Manhattan where I had been the day before. Back in a gallery full of noisy, pretentious people telling me how great Marta's work was and begging me for a scrap of Marta's life when I felt like she had ripped her life away from me. Standing there in the gallery with a forced polite smile, I had heard my mother's voice inside my head fussing, "Keep it up. Your face will freeze that way." I looked around at a room of imploring faces all set in party smiles. Realized mine had been locked in that same joyless grin that was the uniform of the social animal.

I excused myself, politely and with more smiles. Stepped out onto the sidewalk. It was another rainy, gray, dirty, horns-bleating, strangers-bumping-past-without-knowing-you-existed New York day. I found an alley and leaned against the dirty brick and closed my eyes to shut it all out and looked for a calm place in that noisy, noisy place and just found my mind making lists of places Marta might be and reasons she might be there. Opened my eyes and found a street guy trying to go through my pockets. Pushed him away and marched back into the gallery. Turned around, marched back to him and gave him all the bills in my pocket.

"Get really drunk," I told him.

Went back into the gallery where Marta was not and tried to think of it as a place where I was not. Two hours later I stopped smiling and walked the streets alone.

But that was yesterday. Today I was back in Portland and out on the river and couldn't blame my restless mind on the place. My home has been here on the river as long as I can remember. Not the ocean and not the land. The ocean here in the Pacific Northwest is a cold and threatening thing. Beautiful, but not a place fit for man nor beast. And, for me, the land is full of noise, confusion and push-and-shove.

But the river is Mother-Earth-calm when you need that, and puppy-playful when you need an adrenaline rush. That's why my kayak and canoe business is successful: people see the smile on my face when I push their kayak away from my dock, or point out a line for them to follow through boiling white water, know that my smile on the river is as real as the water and the sky. My business is sharing my home and the river is my home.

Not today. Today it was just one more place where Marta was not.

I had been drifting downstream. I pivoted and paddled furiously against the current back to the store. Coming into the dock, I saw my assistant manager Bob stomping down to meet me, the new girl Rue trailing behind him. Bob's arms were chopping at the air as he sputtered non-stop. Two steps behind him, Rue was floating along calmly wearing the beatific smile that looked peaceful but meant she was going to war.

Welcome back to the land.

"Paul, you have got to fire her hippie . . ."

Bob caught himself before adding "ass." Bob is an ex-marine

who had found a fundamentalist church and a fundamentalist wife a month after he came to work here ten years ago. Traded one version of the straight-and-narrow for another, and struggled not to revert when he got mad.

"We don't quit on people, Bob. Never have. Has she killed anybody?"

"No."

"Stolen from us?"

"No."

"Then she's not fired. Make her scrub those old kayaks. Make her pass out flyers for a day."

"Tried that. She picked flowers and handed them out with the flyers. By the end of the day, she was leading a yoga practice in the park."

"And brought in a lot of new business, if I remember right. Even if most of her customers just want to sit in their kayaks and grok the universe until we have to go out and rescue them."

Bob shifted his weight from foot to foot and stared at the ground like he had just been ordered to join the Hare Krishnas.

"What was it this time?" I said. "Giving expired power bars away to the homeless like she did last week?"

"No." He waved a hand at Rue without bringing his eyes up to her. "Look at her."

I looked. Rue was one of those cute otherworldly looking girls, tiny and finely made, looking like a woodland fairy or an angel. Always wearing a quiet smile from her own private world. Always seemed out of focus, like a soft portrait of herself.

"So?"

He waved at her chest and looked away at the water.

"Oh." I saw what he meant. Her shirt was little more than a layer of gauze, and her healthy and clearly female body glowed through it. My angel image of her faded and something more elemental in me felt alive for the first time in months. It took a

31

conscious effort to turn back to Bob.

"Bob, this is Portland, for Pete's sake," I said. "Half the women here don't wear bras. Probably more men than women wear bras here."

Bob's back straightened and I knew I was about to get hell-fire and brimstone. I held up my hand and tried to focus on Rue's eyes.

"Rue, look, you've only been here a few weeks and we've had this talk at least twice."

She interrupted with a big happy smile. "And I enjoyed them both."

I paused and wondered what that meant.

"Well. Just try to put on a sports bra or a thicker shirt when you come to work."

"I was going to. I promise. But when I woke up this morn-ing, the universe told me to put this on. I said, 'Universe, you know I told Paul and Bob I'd wear more.' But the universe said someone would need this today. I go where the universe tells me."

There were a lot of ways Rue was slightly out of focus.

"Yeah, well, ask the universe if you can wear a little more. Grab one of the old tee shirts from the back for today."

She nodded her head vigorously and grinned like I had just complimented her work. I turned back to Bob.

"Better?"

"She's also got to stop renting the old kayaks out for half-price whenever anybody comes in with a sob story about being broke."

Rue started to say something but I put up my hand.

"We're not going to change that," I said to Bob. "We're here to bring people to the river." I turned back to Rue. "Unless it gets out of hand."

I still got the smile from Rue that told me that her mind was busy turning negatives into positives and she was hearing my caution as a compliment. Rue may listen to the universe but she sure doesn't listen to anyone else.

But I was hearing something inside my head, too. Rue's listening to the universe made me realize that I needed to listen to that voice in my own head, the voice that had been telling me for weeks that I had someone I needed to talk to.

Bob said, "She also needs to stop burning incense in the store."

I stood there a second not hearing Bob.

"Work it out," I said. "I've got someplace I need to be."

CHAPTER 7

I drove along Marta's bike route for an hour. Stopped at every convenience store for cups of bad coffee from dark-skinned shopkeepers who turned out to be from Bermuda, Kenya and Montgomery, Alabama. I finally found Marta's bike stop. The tiny concrete block shop squatted old and crumbling in a grove of tulip trees between a working-class neighborhood and a park. Someone was reviving the old shop now. Holes in the walls were patched with homemade care if not skill and the whole thing was painted a bright erratic pink. The letters above the door said, "Kindness Stop" in electric blue. Only in Portland.

"Your accent is beautiful," I said to the man with the neon lime-green Jimmy Buffet t-shirt behind the counter. "Are you by any chance from Leongo?"

"Yes, sah," he said. He wore a big happy-to-be-of-service grin that was several shades brighter than the shirt. "Most beautiful place on earth." He was even taller than me, impossibly thin, with a sadness to his face that showed through the grin.

"I've seen pictures."

"They do not do my home justice. The colors are brighter there, the sun hotter. The air tastes of mango and spices. A man can make a banquet just by breathing; see an art gallery just by opening his eyes. It must have been the garden the good Lord had in mind when he gave the world to men."

"And now you're in Portland, where it rains every day."

He laughed, the hearty laugh expected in the movies when

the simple tropical character needs to show that he is carefree and the customer is oh-so funny and smart.

"It is true, sah, what you say. But it is also true that there is more here in Portland. The people here bring the beauty. There is an artist here who paints magical toys from her childhood, makes them look like a gift from God. Calls her paintings, 'Beauty Everywhere,' and I think that is what makes Portland beautiful. It is a cold and rainy and often gray place. So people bring their own beauty here, and they make beauty everywhere."

"But it's a long ways from Leongo."

"Yes, sah."

I was looking for something to say. "I thought some terrible things happened there a few years back." I was smiling, too, trying to establish a little trust.

"Still happening, even today." His teeth kept the grin but his eyes lost it. "That is why I came here to America. From the most beautiful place on earth to the most wonderful place on earth. How lucky can one man be?"

I took a sip of the coffee. Portland is known for its coffee, but, even here, convenience store coffee was sometimes like drinking dirty water. This was fantastic.

"Great coffee," I said.

"Thank you, sah. Leongo has the best coffee on earth." The polite smile stayed but the eyes were wary. A bike rider came in wearing a jersey with the face of Larry of the Three Stooges painted to look like Mona Lisa. I stepped back as he bought an energy drink and waited until he left. The shopkeeper smiled at the rider but kept his eyes on the man who was staying in his store for no reason.

"This has got to be a great stop for riders, right here on the bike trail like this," I said. I was trying easy banter to reestablish the trust I needed. I've never been much at small talk, or at selling. I felt like a first grader delivering lines in a bad play I didn't understand.

"Yes, sah, that is what makes my day. The bicycle riders come in. They are happy from their ride. They smile, we laugh. I ask them what their mileage is for the day. I write it down in a book I keep under the counter. They come back later, buy food, ask what their mileage was last week, last month. Ask what my book says about them. We laugh. I make money. It is a good life."

"I'm sure it means a lot to the riders. I know it meant a lot to one rider. Do you remember a woman named Marta, used to ride maybe six months ago? Kind of intense, could be a little brusque sometimes?"

His smile now was real. "I called her Fire and Wind. She would blow in here hot, her mind somewhere else, angry at people who tried to talk to her and spoil her concentration with little talk. But for big talk, talk of life and troubles, she always had time and she always wanted to help."

He paused.

"Help people, and tell them what they should do. This was Marta." He shook his finger at me and scowled like Marta.

"That was Marta." I put out my hand. "I'm Marta's husband, Paul."

His eyes grew wide and he grabbed my hand and shook it furiously.

"So you are Paul the Fixer?"

I laughed. "Yeah. Marta called me that sometimes."

"You are the man I am to go to with my problems? You have things for me?"

"No," I laughed, thought it was just a joke of a small shopkeeper. "Don't know much about running convenience stores."

He looked at me a long time.

"Not that business. You are sure you are Paul the Fixer?"

I saw suspicion in his eyes and knew I had made a mistake.

"No, I am Paul the Fixer, I just don't know about this business you're talking about."

His face darkened and he cut me off.

"You would know," he said. "Marta would have told you. Marta would have told her husband about . . . things."

"I don't know. Maybe I am the fixer you need. I just wanted to ask you about—"

"Marta said that bad men will come after her. Do not trust anyone except Paul the Fixer. So, suddenly, I do not remember so much about this Marta. And I do not believe you are Paul the Fixer."

"Well, look, maybe I am the Fixer. Marta used to call me . . ."

"No. Marta would have told you." He put his hand on his phone.

I tried to change topics.

"That's an interesting tattoo." I pointed to three slashes on his forearm, scars rather than narrow tattoo markings but I didn't know what else to call them.

He picked up a rag and covered his arm.

"It is just a mark," he said. "So, do you leave or do I call the police?"

After I left, standing in the parking lot, I looked back through the window. His smile was gone and he was just a man tired of pretending everything's all right with the world.

Late that night, I was drifting between bits of restless sleep and exhausted wakefulness. I turned off the DVD I had been trying to watch. It was an old *Route 66* episode, two clear-eyed young men randomly driving around America finding ways to do the right thing. I watched all the old shows over and over: *Andy Griffith, Gunsmoke, Bill Cosby*. To me, modern TV seemed like freaks laughing at freaks, or freaks shooting freaks. Friends my age laughed at my old-fashioned ways, but I craved the simplicity and goodness of heart of the old shows.

When the last flicker of black and white faded from the TV, I glanced in the mirror at my own face. I saw the same joyless and fearful look as the shopkeeper had shown me.

CHAPTER 8

Friday evening, I locked the door on the kayak shop and stood there thinking of the Leongolian shopkeeper. Thinking of what I might have said to him to get him to talk. Thinking of what he might know, wondering what might be out there.

The key slid out of the lock with a soft click and I heard a louder noise behind me. I froze and wondered if I imagined it. Heard it again. I pretended to study the store window while looking at the reflection of the parking lot at my back and saw someone duck behind a trailer loaded with kayaks. Probably just a punk out looking for anything loose he could pick up. He had picked the wrong time and place. Usually I'd just yell and the punk would run away, but today I felt frustrated and feeble and needed a wrong to right and an ass to kick. The punk had volunteered.

I could see little flashes of movement through the kayaks: one person, not very tall. Someone shook one of the tie-downs. The punk had gone around the back of the trailer to the other side; I went around the front to head him off.

I crouched down at the front of the trailer, ready to come around the corner low and fast and sneaky, but something felt wrong about doing it that way. I had an image of Matt Dillon in the opening scene of every *Gunsmoke* episode: the marshal standing alone in the street tall and sure with his hand by his gun, a hero solving all the problems of the world in one quick second by facing them down with right and justice and a big gun on his side. I stood up straight and stepped strong around the corner of the trailer, hands down and face set in stone and feeling like Matt Dillon.

"Freeze," I yelled, keeping my voice deep and tough.

Rue stood in front of me shaking a tie-down to be sure it was tight. She laughed, looked at me and turned with a smoothness like she was moving from one yoga posture to the next. Smiled and stretched out her arms and one leg into an exaggerated running pose and froze like a kid in a game.

"For crying out loud," I said.

Rue laughed like the universe had given her another joke that was too, too funny for words.

"That was so nice of you," she said. "Play a trick like that just to make me laugh. Good to see you loosening up and having fun."

"Yeah."

We stood there awkwardly for a minute. At least I was awkward. Rue could have stood there smiling forever.

I needed to say something. "What are you doing here? You were off work an hour ago."

"You don't have to pay me. I just want to make sure the tour to the rapids tomorrow to be a good experience for all the first-timers. Make sure everything's locked down tight. Checked the number of kayaks against the roster. We've got two extra."

"I like to have some insurance."

She nodded vigorously. "See, we both want to make the world better for others. It's like we're connected."

"Oh yeah."

"See, look." She pointed at a smudge of black grease on the gunwale of a red kayak. "Maybe tomorrow somebody gets in this kayak, ruins their nice new clothes with this grease. They're bummed out, and they never go back on the river again." She pulled a rag out of the back of her shorts and wiped the grease

40

away. Turned and beamed at me. "Now they get in the kayak with no problem, have a wonderful day, and they love nature for the rest of their lives. I have changed the future, just by being present today."

"So you have." We stood there some more; one of us calm, one awkward. "Well. You need a ride?"

She laughed. "In The Beast?" She pointed at my twenty-year-old Suburban.

"It's not so bad."

"Gets like two miles per gallon. No. If I ride in that thing I'm changing the future another way and poisoning the planet. Plus, it's so old I'm not sure it could make it to my house."

"You know any new cars in better shape than The Beast?"

"No. You do take care of stuff. Nevertheless, I think I'll walk."

"How far?"

"I don't know. Five miles?"

"Lot of walking."

"Lot of opportunity." She stuffed the rag into her waistband. "Five miles of chances to do something good."

She took off walking. Hers was a fine walk; all-woman without any priss or pretense, lean muscles sliding smoothly with confidence and power. She turned her head around, caught me looking and grinned at my expression.

"See?" she seemed to say. "I've brightened your day already."

I cranked up The Beast and went the other way so she wouldn't think I was following her. Drove around aimlessly, but I knew where I'd wind up.

Thirty minutes later, I stood in front of one of Marta's paintings at Larry's gallery, looking for clues and remembering why it mattered so much. There was a noisy milling crowd in the big front room. I eased my way through into the smaller back room that was all-Marta. Larry (or Laurent, if you believed the tastefully hip sign over the front door) planned it that way. Marta was his hot property now; he forced everyone to walk past the new artists he was pushing to get to his star.

The new artist in the front room must have been doing well; the crowd was staying with his paintings and I had Marta's room to myself. I had been through the paintings a hundred times or more, recently, looking for a message that wasn't quite there. I had stepped back and looked at the broad patterns; I had squinted and traced small details repeated from one painting to the next, tried to formulate the meanings of the small changes over the years.

Tonight, I was tired of looking at them as soon as I got here. Wanted to leave but couldn't. Stood in the center of the room and slowly spun around, letting my eyes sweep through Larry's arrangement of Marta's life's work. The early paintings, labeled "blue period" by Larry, came first: bright, creative, fun. Then the brown period of things dark and sad and washed-out. Finally, red: violent and vivid and bloody, fantastic crying trees hacked by long knives and bleeding like people.

I lost the details as I spun and the paintings blurred into a feeling of how our marriage must have looked to Marta: bright and beautiful early, then bored by the man who just wanted things too simple for Marta, then finally the years of disconnected fighting with Marta screaming about passion and me trying constantly to fix things and keep them in order.

I felt dizzy and my eyes grew moist and blurry. I lost my balance and caught myself just before I fell. When I looked up, I saw Detective Martin Ahlstrom standing in the doorway and grinning at me.

"What's the matter?" I said. "Never saw a man dance before?"

"That what I'm looking at?" Ahlstrom said.

"What did you think?"

He took a long several seconds to stare at me unblinking and emotionless while he thought of what to say. "Think I'm looking at man desperate to tell me his secret so I can help him find the love of his life and move on."

"And close your case."

He gave Marta's earliest painting a bored look.

"That, too," he said.

"You know anything about the love of someone else's life?"

His stare seemed to turn inward.

"Know about closing cases." He waved at the painting. "Anyone buy this crap?"

"Only people with human emotions, people who can appreciate a story."

He smiled, just a little one, but probably a belly laugh for him.

"Yeah, that's not me. I can appreciate that these paintings sell for a lot of money now, ever since you and your wife arranged her disappearance." He was back to staring at me now. I looked away from him and focused on Marta's world in the painting. He stepped between me and the painting and locked eyes.

"Or maybe you killed her. Doesn't matter to me. Does to you, though. We both know you're just itching to get it off your chest."

He waited for an answer. This time, it was my turn to think about what I was saying and I said nothing.

Ahlstrom said, "You don't mind if I keep a close eye on your finances, do you?"

"Knock yourself out. You can be like the tax preparation company on TV, let me know if you find any deductions that can save me thousands of dollars."

No smile or laugh this time.

"Don't you have any real cases to work on?" I said. "Portland PD happy to have you spend all your time harassing one guy?"

"They live with it. I take one case at a time, solve it. I'm too close to retirement for them to fire me. They don't like the fact that I'm that way." He paused and looked at the painting. "But until you confess, you're my life."

I had my mouth open to say something when Larry—or Laurent, since we were in his gallery now—walked in carrying a plate of food and a champagne glass. He stopped five feet in front of us when he saw Ahlstrom.

"Detective, I told your chief to lay off my client. The chief agreed. Mr. McClaron is the victim . . . not the suspect."

"Yeah, got the message."

"You looking to get fired?"

"Yeah. The chief said that, too."

Larry jerked his head at the door.

Ahlstrom took in the full Larry/Laurent package. Little purple Alpine hiking hat with a drooping red feather. Paisley ascot, expensive leather suit cut tight to hug his slender figure.

Ahlstrom's nose twitched.

"Goddamned pantywaists run this town," he said as he left.

Larry watched him go.

"Watch out for him," he said. "Chief said he won't follow orders."

"So why do they put up with him?"

"He irritates people, they make mistakes, he gets convictions. Always."

"Always?"

"I asked the chief about the people who are innocent, does he get convictions then? Chief didn't answer. Be careful."

Larry turned and pushed the food and champagne at me.

"Here," he said. "Eat something before you go to jail."

I squinted at his outfit.

"Your girlfriends know you're a pantywaist?" I said.

"Only if it sells paintings," he said. "And the word is 'metrosexual.' People don't trust boring gallery owners or fancy lawyers. Got a gray suit hanging up in the law office."

"I barely change clothes from day to day."

"Yeah, I've noticed. River pants, fishing shirt. They do make those things in different colors you know, so people don't think you're wearing the same clothes every day."

"How do you know I'm not?"

"Only because I know you. You're the man who has to have everything right and clean. I'm more likely to wear dirty clothes than you are. Even your truck has to be spotless. People look at you and see the unpressed shirt and the hands in the pockets and the thick unruly hair and the big smile and they think: good old country boy, nice guy to have a beer with but probably not much going on inside. They don't look close and see the eyes trying to add everything up so it balances exactly so he can shove the world into neat happy rows and columns."

I laughed. "You do sell BS for a living." I didn't want to get into a conversation about me so I changed the topic. "What do you know about Leongo, small country in Africa?"

He shrugged. "Leongo. Kind of today's version of Rwanda or Sierra Leone or Croatia. One of those pitiful little places where everybody kills everybody else because they don't have anything else to do."

"God you're cold. Maybe you should keep living in BS."

Larry didn't laugh. "The law and art don't mean much unless you understand both the bullshit and the reality underneath." He pointed at Marta's painting. "If I come in and see a guy looking at one of Marta's paintings, I've got to decide: Is he just looking for pretty colors to match the couch? If so, I need to push him to something else. Is he looking for an investment? Then I tell him how little her paintings cost a year ago. Once in a while, I catch someone falling into one of her paintings, and I know they're hooked."

"I can understand that."

I was studying a painting and Larry was studying the side of my face.

"Marta was a great artist," he said.

"Yeah."

"No, you don't get my point. She was a great artist because she was never satisfied with anything and never could be. Look at this." He pointed to one of the early paintings, to a detail down in the corner. "Beautiful garden. Now look here." He pointed back at the last painting. "Same garden now has monsters with claws like swords hacking it apart and burning the garden." He paused and looked at me.

"That was Marta. Weird stuff, drugs, hallucinations, turmoil. Made for great art, but had to be hell to live with."

"You see what you want to see," I said, my jaw starting to lock. "You see turmoil, I see passion. Maybe Marta saw the fire in the park when we just saw the park. Maybe without Marta's passion the park becomes just a random bunch of trees."

We both stared at the painting a long time without saying anything.

"In any case," I said, "that's what it feels like now."

Larry nodded. "I know you need to get things to add up in your mind. I'm just saying, old friend, that maybe you've earned a little peace and quiet. Let it go."

I gestured at the painting. "I could never take my eyes off of one of Marta's paintings until I could understand it. I can't walk away now until I understand what's happened."

Larry nodded, patted me on the shoulder and walked away and left me alone. I stared at the painting until my eyes hurt and then I went home for the night.

I undressed and sat on the bed and looked at the dark TV. Picked up the remote and punched the power button and it came up on the old Western channel. Matt Dillon stood with his hand on his gun, ready to solve the problems of Dodge City with one quick draw.

"Aw, shut up," I said and punched the power button again and watched Matt disappear.

CHAPTER 9

I was glad to see Portland fading into my rear view mirror Saturday morning. Portland—my opinion—is one of the world's truly great cities: quirky, comfortable with itself. A city for free thinkers and non-conformists.

But even non-conformists have to march in lockstep to make a city work. Stop when the traffic light is one color, go forward when the powers that be turn it to another color. I looked over at the old Volvo beside me on I84. There was just enough light in the very early morning to read the bumper stickers that covered every square inch of the paint and some of the glass: love your Mother Earth, screw the man, celebrate weirdness. The driver was sixtyish, old enough to be my father, rocking out to the old Eagles' song about taking it easy, his chest-long beard bouncing in time as he shouted about youthful rebellion and the women chasing him, the hand-rolled cigarette miraculously hanging on to his lips. But with all that, we both stayed between the lines someone else had painted for us, and kept our speeds between this number or that, or we would have killed each other. In the city, it was as simple as that. I touched the brim of my river hat and nodded to the old gentleman and he grinned back. I was glad to get off the interstate onto 26.

Rue was up ahead driving a fifteen-passenger van full of rookie paddlers we were taking to their first day of white-water paddling on the Deshutes River. I figured after the way she took ownership last night, she deserved to lead. And I figured she

48

would be more entertaining for our customers than anything on the radio.

But I told her to keep an eye on me in her mirror and let me set the pace. Next to me in The Beast I had one of our staff, Brian, with a cell phone to stay in touch with Rue. I was pulling a trailer with the kayaks. This trip had my name on it and I was responsible for every detail.

Despite that, I could feel the tension of the last six months fall away from me as we passed the last fast food restaurant and entered the Mount Hood National Forest, the magnificent ancient volcano herself filling the sky ahead. Even in Portland, on rare clear days, I go outside and sit on a picnic table in front of the store and stare at her. Most people saw her as a grand old lady, stern and strong with her snow cap looking like hair turned white from carrying the cares of the world. But for me, she had always been a beautiful pale-shouldered young girl, gleaming with hidden strength and beckoning with a promise of something better to anyone who would open their eyes to her.

"Call Rue," I said to Brian. "Remind her to tell the story about John Muir and Mount Hood."

He talked for a minute and hung up.

"She says to tell you that she has your story notes. Has her own notes, too."

"Heaven help us."

The forest was thick and cool as we climbed up the mountain. But somewhere around Government Camp, Rue took an unplanned right and we watched her disappear down the mountain. I pulled off onto what little shoulder there was. Another staffer, Harold, driving the last car in the convoy, pulled in behind me.

"Call Rue," I told Brian. "Tell her to turn around and come join us at an overlook a half-mile on down this road."

Brian came back a minute later.

"Rue says the GPS says she's on the right road. Says your way will take us thirty minutes longer."

"Tell Rue I don't believe in GPSs or UFOs or any other three-letter acronyms. Tell her to join us at the overlook."

When Rue and the passengers climbed out of the van at the overlook, her face still had its smile, but her walk had an attitude and her eyes and her attitude were aiming for me.

"You are costing our customers thirty minutes they could be spending on the water instead of cooped up inside a steel cage on an asphalt road. Brian told me to take the GPS and now you're telling me to ignore it."

I smiled back and Rue stopped when she saw the smile on my face. I waved the thermos of coffee I was holding out at the valley and the forest and the far-away river spread out below us here at the overlook.

"When a GPS can find a view like this," I said, "then I'll believe in a GPS."

She turned and looked and gasped.

"When I was a child, my parents took us to Paris. We went to Notre Dame Cathedral. It was nice. But this," she said, "this is the home of God."

I nodded and we both looked out on the palette of emerald-greens and chocolate-browns and ocean-blues that only one artist could have put together. After about ten minutes, I nodded to Brian.

"Everybody, listen up," he said. People got close and gathered around me.

I pointed out at the river.

"If I ever wonder why I'm alive," I said to the small crowd. "I remember this. Now let's go be part of this beautiful painting."

Rue looked up at me like a puppy. She got in the van, and I followed her down the winding mountain road.

We got to the drop-off at a still point in the river and

unloaded, our rookies bobbing in their kayaks like baby ducks paddling around looking aimlessly for their mother. I paddled to the edge of a pool and nodded and the staff brought everybody over in front of me.

"OK, equipment check," I said. Patted my helmet. "Straps tight. This is a wild river, beautiful and unpredictable and she can hurt you if you're not careful. There is a reason why the ancient legends described wild water as beautiful women who would enchant you with their beauty and destroy you with their power. Don't get caught admiring the water and wind up on the rocks."

We went through the preparations and cautions, practiced the skills we would need. Every other line I gave them warned them to stay with their guide.

At the end, a middle-aged woman I hadn't met raised her hand.

"Are you always smiling?" She was smiling at me, a little coy and maybe flirtatious.

"I don't know," I said. "I've never been accused of that anywhere but around the water." I looked at the sun twinkling off the water and knew the answer. Babies learn to smile by imitating their mothers. My face was taking on the expression I saw in the water.

"OK, let's head out. Brian leads. Don't pass Brian, and stay with your guide."

I held my place in the rear until they were all strung out in front of me. Counted them off in my head for the third of many times today. It was my job to keep them all in front of me and gather stragglers.

My mind flashed back to the cover of *The Catcher in the Rye*. I had been in law school, in line to join my father and his father at McClaron and McClaron in San Francisco when I first read it. Law school was all right for me. Like most kids, I studied

some, partied some, bitched a lot about how stupid it all was.
Like most, I discovered J.D. Salinger's writing, and thought he
was describing my life with every word of alienated youth facing
a prefab future. But his book bothered me more than most of
my friends and I knew Salinger had shown me what I wanted to
be, there in his title: *The Catcher in the Rye*. The man in the field
of rye who catches and protects the children. And my field of
rye was the river.

So my morning filled up with the joy of herding water-borne
cats. We broke for lunch at a little pull-in where a couple of
locals grilled jerk chicken and sweet potatoes for water tourists
like us. The woman who had asked why I was smiling came up
wearing a smile.

"I see where your smile comes from," she said. Without paus-
ing, she put her hand on my forearm. There is something
intimate and sexual about bare skin on bare skin outdoors in
the sunshine, even when the contact is casual.

"I'm so glad you have some joy in your life," she said, and it
seemed to me that her smile started to look like a request. "I'm
so sorry about your recent loss."

I smiled back but took her hand away.

"Thank you," I said, and went off to talk to Brian.

The shadows were starting to lengthen when we came to the
last rapid of the day, a sharp bend in the river with boiling
water on one side and a calm path on the other. I counted
again; everyone was accounted for.

The woman raised her water bottle to me in a toast. The
bottle slipped out of her hand, fell into the river and I grimaced
and went to get it for her. A boy who had been paddling next to
her went to get it, too. I backed off.

Then I saw that he wasn't gaining on the bottle and I saw
why: the bottle was being pulled to the wild side of the river,

toward a water feature called a hydraulic, sort of a vertical whirlpool that would pull you under over and over until you drowned.

"Leave it," I yelled.

He smiled back. "I've got it." He kept paddling.

I had the advantage of experience, but he had a head start. He suddenly realized he was going much faster than he was paddling, and froze in mid-stroke. He looked like a cartoon character still running off the cliff after his feet had stopped.

He hit a rock, hung up, and I thought I was going to get to him at the rock. But his kayak spun free and now he was backwards, facing me with a horrified and helpless look.

"Hold on," I yelled. I beat the water and knew it would be close. His kayak reached the small waterfall at the hydraulic and I saw the boat tip as the water pounded the nose of the boat under. If the waterfall caught him, it would slam him against the rocks on the bottom before letting him up just to slam him down again and again.

The waterfall poured into his cockpit as I reached him. I dropped my paddle and grabbed him with both hands, yanked him out of his kayak, and threw him beyond the rapids to safety. I saw him swimming madly for calm water as the hydraulic hit me.

The waterfall tore me out of my kayak. I pulled myself into a tight ball but the water slammed my back into the rocks on the bottom and I felt like my spine had exploded. I clawed into the up-flow of water coming off of the rocks. I burst through to the surface and covered my head to get a second's worth of air before I was hammered down again. This time I was pile-driven into the rocks headfirst. The helmet didn't help much.

I felt my arms and legs float loose and helpless. I remembered hitting my head one more time, and I remembered feeling detached and calm.

★ ★ ★ ★ ★

I wish I could say that I thought of Marta or saw a blinding light or had some insight for the ages. Instead, I was back on the river with my dad the first time he took me fishing. I felt sunshine seeping through my skin to nourish me and I smelled the water. I remembered what it was like to catch that first small fish, hold it up to my father, see his pride. I wanted to hold onto that fish forever.

"If you take him home," said my father, "he'll be dead by nightfall. Hold him in your heart, and you will have him until your dying moment." He took the fish off my hook and put him in my hands. I saw the fish shimmer in front of me now.

"Now set him free," I heard my father's voice say. "He has more living to do."

Strong arms ripped me out of the water and into the sky. I felt like I was watching a movie and admired the effect the director had come up with: sparkling water drops suspended in a bright blue sky. Something burst into the movie frame: a face like a demon awakened from hell: angry, determined, mouth tight and eyes hard. Rue without the smile.

She yanked me out into smooth water and my vision cleared. She crossed an arm over my chest and dragged me to a kayak so fast I thought we were leaving a wake.

"Where does it hurt?" she shouted. Her face was inches in front of mine, eyes searching my face, her hands holding me up by the straps of my life vest as she walked backwards across the rocks on the shallow bottom, pulling me with her. More hands grabbed me and secured me to the deck of a kayak.

"Careful," Rue said. "Don't move him until we know where he's hurt."

Rue's face filled my sky like the sun and her smile was coming back as she touched me looking for breaks and injuries. I knew I had to answer her.

"I feel wondrous," I said. I smiled and then I passed out.

CHAPTER 10

I woke up on the bank at the landing, strapped to the foredeck of a kayak with bungee cords to keep me immobile. My head throbbed and my back felt like a pretzel and I said, "Wow."

"Rue, he's waking up."

The face of smiling Rue floated into my vision. "Is the little boy ready to tell Mama where he skinned his knee?"

"Back's a little sore and I have a headache. Nothing that won't be OK if you will just tell the Lilliputians to cut me loose and let me walk it off."

"Next time you'll be walking is when you come out of the local hospital. We're going to load you in Kenny's car and I'm going to take you there now."

I pushed to sit up.

"Cut me loose here, and I'll walk to the car. But we're not going to any hospital."

"We'll carry you."

Brian's head floated into view.

"I wouldn't argue," he said. "The way she threw you around in the river, I'd do what she says." His head turned to Rue and he smiled. "How'd a cute little thing like you get so strong?"

"Yoga. Lots of yoga."

He laughed. "Must be yoga with fifty pound weights."

She ignored him.

"Really, Paul. You need to get checked out."

"Really, Rue, I'm fine other than feeling like a deer strapped to the hood of a hunter's truck. Cut me loose and let's all go home."

I strained at the cords and almost flipped the kayak. Rue put her hand on my head.

"Alright," she said. "My brain thinks you need to get to a hospital, but the universe is telling me to listen to you. How about this? We load you into Kenny's car, drive you to Portland. If you don't feel really OK by the time we get there, you promise to let us get you checked out."

I looked at her. It was hard not to smile back, and something about her made me want to agree to anything she wanted.

But I am ornery by nature. "And if I say no?"

She smiled even sweeter, bent down and played with my hair.

"Plan B is this: we hit you over the head with a rock until you pass out, take you to the hospital and tell them the river did it. What about Plan A now?"

"Deal."

I found a few new aches and pains as they loaded me into Kenny's car, the seat reclined so I could lie flat. Kenny fished his car keys out of his shorts. Rue snatched them out of his hand.

"I'm driving. You get your car back when Paul's home safe. Get in the back and let's get going."

I remember the car pulling away from the river, and I remember waking up sometime later, leaning up, and watching the mountain float into my sight, move across it and disappear as we rounded a broad curve. The next thing I remembered was a big young Samoan man with a huge head bending over me. The name tag on his white jacket had more vowels than Portland had coffee shops.

"Hey, Sleeping Beauty," said Rue's voice behind the giant.

I looked past him to Rue.

"I never agreed to a hospital."

57

She shrugged. "I asked you if you objected while you were passed out. You didn't say anything, so I took that as a yes."

Kenny's voice was somewhere in the room. "Paul, don't ever let her drive anything faster than a kayak again. Once you passed out, she drove my little car like it was a Formula One racer. We made the two and a half hour trip in an hour and a half, sliding through every curve on the road."

"I was afraid you'd wake up before we got here," Rue said, "and I'd have to listen to you argue about getting checked out."

I smiled. The giant doctor ran tests, shuffled me from one piece of expensive hospital equipment to another. Then Rue and I sat alone in a little curtained-off space and we were suddenly awkward and not sure of what to say to each other. After enough time for a million words to pass between us, but nothing but meaningless little small talk, the doctor finally came back in.

"OK, I'm going to let you go. You're lucky. A lot of bumps and bruises. You're going to be pretty sore for a long time. You've got a mild concussion." He turned to Rue. "Don't let him sleep for more than a couple of hours at a time tonight. If you can't wake him up, get him back here."

"Oh no," I said to the doctor. "She's not—we're not a couple. I have a wife."

The doctor looked at Rue's expression and shrugged.

CHAPTER 11

I got out of Kenny's car at my house. I felt like a tin man with rusted hinges, but I smiled and acted like it was no big deal.

"Man, I feel good now," I said. "May have to get more of whatever drug that wrestler/doctor gave me."

"Nice try," said Rue, pulling her day pack out of the back. "You've got a nurse tonight, whether you like it or not."

"No, I'm fine." I did a jumping jack to show Rue how healthy I was. I felt like an illustration in an anatomy book with every muscle outlined in pain, but I kept smiling.

She didn't move.

She could be stubborn. So could I.

"I'm a grown man," I said, losing the smile. "I can take care of myself."

I thought I was about to get that scary Rue look I had seen at the river, but Kenny intervened.

"Look, Rue, I've got about an hour's drive back to my house. How about if I give Paul a call when I get there. My wife Claire gets up early, so she can call him a couple of hours after that. If he answers those two calls we declare him cured."

Rue was staring off into space, listening, but not to either Kenny or me.

"OK," she said. "The universe says you're OK." She turned to Kenny. "But you call him just the same. And call me if he doesn't answer."

"Thank you, universe," I said. I nodded at Rue. "And thank

59

you, Dr. Ben Casey."

Rue threw her pack over her shoulder. "I'll check on you tomorrow." She turned to walk away and said over her shoulder, "And I wouldn't be Ben Casey, I'd be Maggie. Surprised that I know the old TV shows? I'm full of surprises. And I'm a girl doctor." She turned her head back to me and flashed a grin. "Or hadn't you noticed." Walked away and left Kenny and me watching her go.

Kenny drove away and I stood on the sidewalk waving and smiling. As soon as he disappeared around the corner, I slumped like a sack of dirty laundry. It took me five aching minutes to make the walk to my front door and fish the key out from its hiding place. I prayed for enough strength to unlock the door, collapse onto the living room couch, and never move again.

I stepped into the house with my head down and made it to the couch. Something was wrong. The couch was upside down, the fabric on the bottom cut open and hanging loose. I raised my eyes slowly. Drawers dumped. Every piece of furniture turned upside down and cut open. The carpet was sliced in a long diagonal slash and pulled open.

For once, I wished I carried a gun. I stood and listened. Backed out to the porch and pulled out my cell phone to call the police, then hesitated. Something didn't make sense. I put one foot back into the house and peeked in.

Hanging on the wall untouched was my big screen TV, my one expensive indulgence in the house. The theater chairs in front of the TV were turned upside down and split open like everything else, but the TV was untouched.

I put my phone back in my pocket. This wasn't the kind of break-in to report to the police. I stood there for a minute, then decided I had been hanging around Rue too much listening to voices in my head. My good citizen voice told the universe to shut up, and I called 9-1-1 and was told to wait for the police.

The good citizen voice wasn't strong enough for that. I stepped back in and listened some more. Tip-toed to the patio door and pried out the broomstick I use to block the sliding door. Tried to remember how we were taught to hold a stick in the one martial arts class I took, and settled for gripping it like Mickey Mantle gripped a baseball bat.

I crept around the downstairs. Same pointless destruction throughout, but nothing missing. I went up through the bedrooms on the second floor. The mattresses were ripped open, drawers dumped out. The third floor had Marta's studio and my office.

My office had received the full treatment: every book was off the shelves and thrown on a pile. My files were on the floor.

Most of my files. I keep financial records in purple folders. There were no purple folders. I looked at my desk. My laptop was gone.

Marta's studio was untouched. Her last painting stood where I had found it six months ago. I hadn't looked at it for a long time. I stared at it now, but Paul the Practical Man had no answers, just a stupid beaming grin.

"If you're so smart—" I started to say to stupid Paul. There was a noise downstairs.

I tightened my grip on the broomstick and crept down the stairs. The last step on the first floor had a creak in it; I was looking down to step over it. Didn't see the shadow on the wall until I was turning the corner and came face to face with a man.

"Freeze," we both yelled and jumped back. I had a broomstick. He had a gun.

A gun in a trembling hand and a scared, sweaty, young face. And a blue uniform.

"It's OK, officer," I said. I put the stick down carefully. I watched the finger on the gun twitching.

"I'm the homeowner," I said. "I called you guys." I put my hands up slowly.

"Sure you did," he said.

"Look, I can prove it."

I started dropping my right hand to my wallet. More twitching. I stopped.

"Can I get my wallet out?"

He thought about it.

"Sure. But be careful."

I very, very slowly reached back and pulled my wallet out. Another officer came in from the kitchen. He was older.

"Jeez, Jones," he said. He put his hand on the kid's gun and lowered it. I opened my wallet and showed him my license.

"How about that, Jones? This notorious felon you just got the drop on happens to live here. Think you'll have to wait for your second day on the job to shoot your first criminal."

Jones holstered his gun.

"You're supposed to wait for us," he said. "There could be dangerous perps still in the house."

"Yeah." I was too tired to say what I thought.

"I need you to wait on the porch, sir, while we secure the domicile."

The older cop shook his head. "I'll stay down in this part of the domicile with Mr. McClaron and get the report started while you secure the rest of the domicile."

Jones got tight-lipped and started up the stairs.

"Jones," said the older cop. Jones stopped and turned around.

"Don't shoot the domicile."

Jones stood up straight and offended and marched up the stairs like his gun had been shoved up his butt.

I started to turn over a chair to sit down.

"No, sir," said the cop. "I'm sorry, but we need you to leave things as they are until the crime scene guys get here."

"Let's try the kitchen," I said. We walked into the kitchen together. "Mind if I make coffee?"

He hesitated and I gave him a heartfelt tired look.

"Sure," he said. "All the crime scene boys will do is take pictures that will just get thrown in a file and forgotten anyway. Let me get my laptop. My name's Meyer, by the way."

I put on the coffee and sat a couple of chairs upright at the table. I was sitting at the table when Jones stepped out the front door just as Meyer came back in and we got started. We were sitting at the table drinking coffee and entering my address into the forms on his laptop for the third time when a detective walked in.

"Novack," he said as he bounded over and stuck out his hand. He had a big toothy grin and leading man good looks. I put my hand out and he jerked my arm up and down like it was an exercise machine and he had to get twenty reps done in ten seconds. What I got was shooting pain from my fingers to my neck. He turned loose and I flopped my arm onto the table.

"Glad to meet you, sir," he said. The smile was so big and so fixed I wanted to reach up and see if it peeled off.

"I hope Officer Meyer and his partner are treating you well." He looked at his watch. "Fourteen minutes since the call. Make sure you get that in the report, Meyer." Looked back at me. "We try to have an investigator on the scene within twenty minutes. I try to make fifteen."

"Very . . . commendable," I said. I didn't know what else to say.

"Thank you, sir. The Portland Police Department wants you to know that we take the 'serve' part of our motto seriously."

"I'll write a letter to the editor thanking you." I was tired and it was more sarcastic than I meant. Didn't matter.

"Would you, sir? That would be so helpful."

"Yeah, sure. Look, do you think there's any chance of catching whoever did this?"

"We'll do our best, sir."

"I'm sure you will. What are the chances?"

He hitched up his pants and put a concerned look on his face. Turned around slowly, studied the living room for a second, and turned back.

"Well, sir, we'll do our best, but it looks like just another typical drug robbery. Junkies—I mean, unfortunate citizens with a drug dependency—break into places at random, looking for drugs or cash or whatever they can hock easily." The smile came back. "But you can be sure we'll keep careful records of your incident so we can add it to our statistics and document the severity of this troubling national problem."

I looked at Meyer and he had the expressionless look of a man who had something to say and couldn't say it.

"Comforting," I said. Meyer smiled and put his head down where Novack couldn't see it.

There was a harsh laugh at the door.

"Looks like a pretty organized drug addict to me." Ahlstrom was leaning in the doorway.

Novack turned and you could almost hear him hiss. "This is my case."

"Sure it is." Ahlstrom walked around the room ignoring us and looking at everything else.

"They had me on a stupid bank robbery," he said. "Heard the address and thought I'd come down here and say hi. Haven't seen you in a while." He forced a smile but it looked like a grimace.

Novack said, "You can't just walk off a bank robbery."

Ahlstrom studied the coffee pot. "Bank robbers always get caught anyway. Besides, you know the FBI's going to jump in and take the case."

Ahlstrom waved at the coffee pot. "Shouldn't let Mr. Mc-

Claron make coffee and mess up your crime scene." He waggled a finger at Novack. "You broke the rules. Shame, shame."

Novack said, "Why don't you—?"

"So what was taken?" said Ahlstrom.

Meyer said, "Just a laptop." For some reason, I didn't want to tell them about the financial records.

Ahlstrom stared at me while Meyer was talking. "There was something more."

"What?" said Novack.

Ahlstrom was bent over looking at the back door. "Don't know that." He straightened up and looked back at me, this time with his real grin. "Yet."

Jones walked back in from out on the street.

"Hey, I've got something. The neighbor across the street said he saw something. Said he saw a dark-skinned guy around the house earlier."

"Figures," said Novack. "Even here in liberal Portland, everybody assumes the perp is always a black guy."

"That what the neighbor said, black?" said Ahlstrom.

"No," said Jones. "Just 'dark-skinned.' Maybe black, Hispanic, wasn't sure."

Ahlstrom looked at me.

"You're pretty dark-skinned."

Novack snorted. "Now you're accusing the victim. Really, Ahlstrom, your community relations skills have got you in trouble before. I'd suggest you walk away."

Meyer shook his head at me and waved his hand at Ahlstrom and Novack. "Beauty and the Beast, we used to call them, back when they were partners." He turned to Ahlstrom. "But really, detective, why would Mr. McClaron trash his own house?"

Ahlstrom stared at me.

"Don't know. Mr. McClaron likes making up crimes. Or covering them up."

Novack snorted again. "Watch out for this guy," he said to me. "He's crazy and he's the one who likes to make things up."

"Nobody walks away guilty on my watch," said Ahlstrom.

"And everybody's guilty," said Novack. "At least in this guy's mind." He stepped over and poked Ahlstrom in the shoulder. Ahlstrom winced. "Including himself." Poked him again and Ahlstrom backed away.

Novack said, "See, he thinks he's a tough detective, but he can't stand to be touched or made fun of."

Meyer watched and didn't interfere.

Novack said, "He thinks everybody's a guilty little chicken-shit like he is, wants to see them punished because he's afraid of all the things he thinks he's guilty of. Ashamed of himself." Poked him again. "Why he has to get a conviction on every case he takes, no matter what. Isn't that right, Ahlstrom?"

He kept poking him. I thought Ahlstrom would fight back but he didn't.

"Enough," I said. I stepped between them. "Nobody gets picked on in my house."

Novack shrugged and backed away.

Ahlstrom was beaming up at me like I was his savior.

CHAPTER 12

It took most of the night and a lot of the next day to finish with the police and put the house back together enough for a compulsive like me to feel comfortable falling asleep. When I woke up, the sky out my window was pearl-gray and I thought it was early morning.

I lay still and felt pretty good, thinking about getting up and getting things done in the day ahead. There was a small bird tapping on the outside of the house downstairs: a constant tap-tap-tap that never varied in cadence or volume. I threw off the covers and started to get out of bed to shoo the bird away. My body, in a jagged symphony of cramps, ripping aches and screaming shooting pains, brought the last two days back to me. I lay back down and stayed as still as I could.

The bird wouldn't stay still and I imagined holes being pecked in the woodwork. I pushed one leg over the bed, then the other. I felt like an old man trying to do a young man's robot dance: move one part of my body carefully, pause, move another. Prayed that the grimace on my face would go away before my face hardened permanently that way.

"Damned old fool." I loosened up enough to fish a pair of river shorts off the floor and pull them on and head down the stairs.

The tapping was coming from the front door. I rapped on the door once to scare the bird away. The bird rapped back once. I rapped twice. The bird rapped shave-and-a-haircut and I stood there. I opened the door.

The small bird was Rue, smiling and holding up a bottle of wine. She stared at me like she was looking at a wonder of nature, and I felt even more naked than I almost was.

"You're a walking advertisement for the outdoor life." She pushed past me, lightly brushing against my chest for an instant. Looked at the long rip in the carpet but said nothing.

"How long have you been knocking on the door?" I said.

"Little while."

"You know, there's a doorbell."

She made a face. "I don't like machines. The universe wants me to be a gentling force. So I don't want to slam an electronic 'bong' in people's ears, or jolt them with a loud banging knock. I just give them a gentle tapping, let them slowly and naturally become aware of my presence. Good rhythm practice, too."

I nodded at the bottle. "Wine for breakfast?"

"What time do you think it is?"

I studied the light. "Five, six a.m."

"Try seven p.m. Sunday. Do I have to ask you the year to test your brain function?"

"No," I stood there for a minute, putting the pieces of the last couple of days back together.

"How's the head?" she said.

I shook my head from side to side. Nothing rattled or came loose.

"Not bad," I said. "Little groggy. Not much of a headache."

She nodded. "And the body?"

It seemed like more of a personal question than it was and I wished that I had a shirt on.

"I think I have one muscle somewhere in my big toe that's not screaming. That what the wine is supposed to cure?"

"No." She held the bottle up chest-high. "That's the reward."

I looked at Rue and the bottle and wondered which one was

the reward and what the reward was for.

"The work will be the cure. The wine is after you do the work." She looked around. "Do you have a wood floor anywhere?"

"Sure. Kitchen."

"Come on."

"Let me get a shirt on. Be there in a minute."

I heard her voice as I went up the stairs.

"Nothing fancy. Nothing you can't sweat in."

I pulled a t-shirt out of my dresser. Caught a glimpse of myself in the mirror. Put on deodorant, a better shirt, combed my hair and brushed my teeth.

Rue was sitting in Lotus Pose on my kitchen floor, her hands folded in front in Namaste. Eyes half-closed in a way that was sleepy, confident and sexy. She had pushed the kitchen table back, and put on a Miles Davis album on my old turntable. Miles' smoky, unhurried rhythm filled the room. She motioned me to the empty floor.

"Do what I do."

I laughed.

"I can't even sit like that right now."

She stood up and put her hands on my shoulders. It was the first time she had touched me—at least when she wasn't saving my life—and I felt a current flow between us. We looked at each other for a long moment.

She shook it off.

"OK, let's touch your toes."

I bent over a little and she guided my back as far as it would go.

"Then let's touch your knees instead. Hold it here for a few seconds and concentrate on your breathing. Feel the toxins flowing out of your muscles and the healing flowing in."

I hung there. On each exhale, she would push my shoulders

down softly until my hands were almost to my feet.

"Very good," she said, guiding me back up. She sat me down and pulled my legs apart until the soles of my feet were touching. Placed her hands on my knees and rocked them slowly up and down.

She dropped her voice into an easy whisper. "This is the Butterfly Pose." After a few seconds of rocking, she said, "We're going to go deeper."

She put her hands on my shoulders and wrapped her legs around me. Sitting in my lap with her face an inch in front of me, she whispered, "Breathe," and I felt her breath wash over my face.

She was as light as a feather in my lap but she kept shifting her weight from my shoulders to my legs until my legs were almost flat on the floor. I could feel myself stir and hoped she wasn't looking at my shorts.

She unwrapped herself and guided me into a twist, then into another pose. Twenty minutes later, we finished the last Sun Salutation and I lay on my back for Shavasana meditation while Rue sat cross-legged and watched over me. After a few minutes, she guided me back up.

"What hurts now?" she said.

"Everything," I said. "But much less."

"Do that every day." She poured me a tall glass of water. "Drink this first." She pointed at the wine. "Then this."

"Medicine?"

I drank the water while she poured the wine. We took our glasses into the living room. I looked at the couch and the chair. Decided I needed to sit in the chair. She sat on the arm.

Miles was playing a slow, sad song about the things you needed but could not have. I got up to change the album and the mood. I looked at my collection of Keb' Mo', Crosby, Stills, Nash and Young and Joni Mitchell. It all looked too romantic right now, so I punched a radio station. I went back and sat on the couch. Rue came over and sat beside me. I gave up.

"Rue, look," I said. "I can't tell you how much I appreciate this. This, and that little matter of saving my life yesterday."

She shook her head.

"You don't have to thank me. The universe gave me that opportunity. And now that she—the universe is decidedly a she—gave me that opportunity, I am obligated to you."

"You're obligated to me?"

She nodded emphatically. "The giver must always be grateful. I am responsible for you now."

"Well, that's . . . nice. But, I'm glad you talked about obligations. I have a wife who I'm responsible for. Well, not exactly responsible. But I am married, Rue. And I will stay married. I don't quit on people."

She smiled up at me. "You have such a strength to you, and such kindness and certainty. You are like a rock. I sensed that the first day I met you."

"I don't feel like a rock right now, but thanks."

"You are. And the rock doesn't change, no matter what changes around him. See, look, you are still married in your heart, even after your wife is . . ." she paused, looking for the right word, "transitioned."

I didn't say anything.

"But even a rock can crack from too much pressure. The rocks in the river need the water."

"Rue, I'm sorry. I won't try to tell you I'm not attracted to you, but . . ."

She giggled. "Not after Butterfly Pose. Parts of you loosened up quite well."

I moved down the couch and she followed.

"Well, jeez, I am a guy, after all. Put a good-looking young woman in my lap and things happen."

"Aw, now you're trying to sweet-talk me."

"But even if I weren't married—which I am—there is that matter of working together."

She laughed.

"I think you've got me wrong. I'm not looking for a boyfriend. I stopped doing the girlfriend thing a few years back."

I felt like a fool for even suggesting anything. I always seemed to read the signals wrong on women. Rue was just being a friend.

My friend snuggled into my shoulder.

"No, I'm not a girlfriend, I'm a healer. The universe guides me to someone who needs me. I stay with them for six months. I heal them. Then it's time for me to move on."

"Wasn't there a movie about that?"

"That's how the universe showed me my destiny. Gave me that old movie on TV on a night when my life was falling apart and I needed direction. I've followed where she has led me since then."

She looked up at me and her hand rubbed my arm.

"I sense a rip in your aura, a pain that cuts to your soul. You need someone to help you lift your burden."

I suddenly felt tired and sad and weary and in need of comfort and gentleness and strength. I leaned down and kissed Rue on the top of her head.

When I woke up, the windows were gray again. I was still on the couch and Rue was still nuzzled next to me. She snored, a raucous, ripping, uninhibited man-snore that was sweet coming from such a little girl. She made one last snort and her eyes opened. She smiled up at me and wiped the corner of her mouth. She looked up at the clock.

"The baby slept all night," she said.

She laughed and patted me on the head and stood up.

"And that's all baby did," she said. "You kissed me on the

head, mumbled something like, 'Please,' and went out like a light."

She picked up her bag.

"Rue, look," I said. "Thank you for everything. I'm sorry it's not going to work out."

She laughed. "Yeah, I know, it's not me, it's you. I understand."

She walked over, leaned down and kissed me on the top of my head.

"Really, I do understand."

Turned and walked out the door.

CHAPTER 13

Standing at the window, I watched Rue walk away and wondered what I was doing and why I was doing it. I needed something simple and clear that needed to be done now. There was nothing to do at the shop: it was Monday, the one day of the week that the shop is closed. I could go there, but today I felt like I would be out of place even there.

I was wide awake now. The soreness was leaving me, thanks to Rue. I had too much energy to sit and watch an old movie.

I made coffee and warmed up a microwave breakfast biscuit and took them both out to my woodshop. My intruders seemed to have missed this space—no evidence they'd even looked inside—and I found myself idly wondering why. But only for a moment.

There was a half-finished wooden frame from an old-style kayak up on a bench. My idea was to build it with nothing but hand tools from the nineteenth century, bring it in and hang it on the shop wall as a reminder of craftsmanship and dedication to doing things right.

I picked up a spar and sighted down it. Almost straight. Almost smooth. The custom mill I get my wood from delivers a good product and takes their work seriously.

So do I. I clamped the wood in place and picked up a sanding block. Soon I was sweating and mindless, feeling the wood become true and my mind become clear. I paused and smiled.

I glanced out the window, up to the big north window in

Marta's studio. Thought about marriages and how they worked, the way the partners fill gaps in each other like carefully-notched woodwork. In our marriage, I handled the clear and the direct. I was the one to come up with the answers.

Marta handled the weird and spent her time wrestling with her anger and the questions with no answers. Hers was the world of passion and exasperation, filled with violent and often pointless flailing at anything that outraged her at the moment.

The day that I brought the wood home for this kayak, I was standing where I stood today, sorting the wood, seeing in my mind's eye how it would all fit together. There was a crash and I looked at the house in time to see a painting and shards of glass raining down on the yard from Marta's window, Marta standing at the hole screaming. I ran up the stairs and grabbed her before she fell out the broken window.

"I don't love it," she screamed, as if I was supposed to understand that. "I have to find something to love." She pushed me away and ran out of the house. I replaced the window with glass strong enough not to break the next time. When she came home a week later, she was bruised and dirty and smelled of smoke and body odors. We sat in the kitchen and she glared across the table at me and snarled, "Don't ask."

But, through it all, I stood in awe of her ability to live with the weirdness of the world, to somehow sort it all out and turn it into beautiful paintings.

So, if a marriage is a complex dance of filling gaps, after the partner is gone, you find yourself lost, trying to grow ways to fill in those gaps for yourself. Today, there was more weirdness in my world than I could handle by myself. I caught myself wondering if today would be the day that Marta came back; imagined sitting with her in the kitchen asking her what to do about Ahlstrom and Rue. Especially Rue. I laughed at myself, laughed about the fact that I needed advice from Marta even now about whether to move on with my life without her.

"Big dummy," I said to myself. Flashed back to a time in childhood when I was the big, shaggy-haired, good-natured kid in school that kids would pick on because they knew I wouldn't hit back. Picked up the spar again and felt like it was my only friend.

I sighted down the spar, saw that it was straight and smooth now and knew that I had done right by the material. I set the spar down in its place on the frame and knew that if I pushed down with the slightest effort, it would click into place and become part of the boat. I also knew that I needed more of an answer today than the wood could provide.

There was only one dark-skinned man who I had had a conflict with lately. I showered, shaved, hopped in the car and drove back to the Leongolian convenience store. There were three cyclists bunched at the counter, laughing with the Leongolian. He followed me with his eyes while his mouth laughed and joked with them. They left with him telling them that they should ride twice as much and buy three times as much.

I poured a cup of coffee and approached the counter.

"You are not welcome here," he said. He had one hand under the counter.

"You are not welcome in my house," I said. I leaned across the counter. He did not back down.

"It was a small matter," he said.

I stared at him. He shrugged.

"Marta invited me. We had coffee. Marta gave me some money for . . . other people. That is all."

"Marta was there?"

"Of course."

"You know where Marta is?"

Now he stared at me.

"This was a long time ago."

I paused. "You weren't there yesterday?"

"Of course not. Marta is no longer here, no?"

More staring from both of us.

"I know who you are," he finally said. "I asked. I know now that you are Marta's husband. I still do not believe that you are Paul the Fixer that I am to watch for."

"I told you last time, Marta used to call me 'Paul the Fixer' sometimes."

"It is not important. Marta also told me once that she did not want you involved. So, I think the fixer she is sending is not her husband, but is this kind of fixer." He put his finger on his nose and pushed it to the side.

"So you think the fixer is like a wise guy, some shadowy crook with connections?"

He thought a minute. "I think you are probably a nice man who does not need to be involved in this. And you are not the fixer."

I tried to look at him hard like a cop on TV. "So you did not break into my house the other day?"

His eyes grew wide.

"Someone broke into your house?"

"Someone broke into my house and tore it up looking for something and I think you know who and why."

"I do not know you," he said. He scanned the parking lot and looked up and down the street. "Please, do not come back here. Do not lead them here. Do not come back here."

A Portland police officer walked in and studied the awkward silence between us.

"Thanks for the coffee," I said, and left.

CHAPTER 14

"No, trust me, you want to do this."

The voice on the other end of the phone was Larry, which meant that I probably wouldn't enjoy whatever this was turning into.

"Look, Larry," I said. "I'll go to dinner with you and Sheila but . . ."

"Tiffany. Don't call her Sheila and get me in trouble like you did when you called Sheila, Melanie."

"Tiffany. Can you get your girlfriends to wear nametags so I can keep them straight? Anyway, I'll be glad to go to dinner. I just want to be sure this isn't going to turn into another one of your blind dates."

"Wouldn't think of it," he said, in a voice that made me think that was exactly what he was thinking.

It was Friday morning at the shop. I was sitting cross-legged on the floor, talking to Larry on my cell while I was looking at a new-model kayak that had just been delivered. Rue was standing on the other side of the boat, slowly running her hands up and down the side, making friends with the boat.

"Sheila-Tiffany's not going to have a friend come along at the last minute?" I said. "Not going to have a promising young artist with 38DD's happen to bump into us and tell me how much she'd just love for me to teach her how to paddle, winking and licking her lips while she says it?"

Rue was close enough to hear. She giggled. "Might be fun.

The kayak, I mean."

I shifted away so she couldn't hear, at least not as well. She walked away and smiled back over her shoulder at my reaction. I sat down on the hardwood floor with my back to the wall.

"Hey now, that was Amber," said Larry. "You should have taken her up on that."

"I told you," I said to Larry but loud enough for Rue to hear, too. "I'm still married."

"Were married. Need to move on," he said. "We've been through this before. I promise. No tricks. Just calling to tell you to dress up. Dress a little formal, maybe a little dark. We're going someplace nice."

"We usually go to a barbecue joint unless your girl-of-the-week is a vegetarian."

"Better than that tonight. Special place. Pick you up at seven. Remember, formal."

He was gone without a goodbye and I sat on the floor watching Rue unpack a display of water bottles. She would take a bottle out of the box, hang it up, give the bottle a Namaste greeting, then lay one hand on the bottle, close her eyes and tell the bottle what wonderful adventures it would have in its life. Every bottle had its own story. Bob passed behind her and shook his head but didn't say anything.

Rue and I had shared an amiable week. She kept finding little chores to do around me. Every time I looked up, she was ten feet away. She would smile her mother-hen smile. I would smile back. I could live with that. Nothing wrong with smiling.

So, this Friday, after the call was finished, we smiled the day away and I went home to wait for Larry and his girl X who I hoped wouldn't be bringing a girl Y for me. I looked in my closet and tried to figure out what I had that was formal and dark. I did have one black suit, last worn to an uncle's funeral more than ten years ago. I pulled it out from where it was hiding in the back and held it up. Wondered for a minute if it would fit, then smiled at myself. I'm pretty compulsive about my weight and conditioning. People look at me and see a shaggy, shambling man, head down, clothes loose and casual, and never guess that I've seen a day of exercise in my life. Most would guess I'm about six-two, one eighty and soft. But I'm a solid six-four, two-oh-five. Every morning starts with a hundred push-ups and a hundred crunches and twenty minutes of kick boxing, all done in private, before I take to the water for my morning paddle. When my weight creeps up to two-twelve, the pushups and crunches go up to one-fifty and lunches become salads.

So the suit would still fit me fine. The question was whether I would fit the suit; if I would spend the whole evening feeling like I was at a funeral instead of relaxing. I voted for relaxing and put the suit back in its corner.

I took down the navy blazer that was my standard lecturing-at-a-museum coat. Put it on over my khaki quick-dry river pants and denim shirt. That was as formal as Larry would get from me tonight. And if there was a girl Y waiting for me tonight, well, she was going to be disappointed anyway.

My house has a front porch with a wooden swing and a couple of rocking chairs, like Andy's house on the *Andy Griffith Show*. I was sitting on the swing, picking out one of Keb' Mo's riffs on an old guitar when Larry's limo eased in and filled up the curb in front of my house. I put the guitar in the house and locked up.

"Jeez," said Larry as I walked up. "That's formal?"

"Got shoes on and everything."

"I think he looks great," said the girl on the seat next to Larry. She was a tall country-curvy blonde with a Southern drawl and a big happy smile.

"I like dress up," she said, "but I like it because I like it. Not because somebody tells me to. And I like a man who doesn't let anybody else tell him how to dress." She stuck her hand out. "Tiffany." She shook hard and firm, more like a longshoreman than a Tiffany. I liked her.

I smiled back at her, sat down in the jump seat and jerked a thumb at Larry and said to Tiffany, "What you going to do when Larry here tries to tell you what to do?"

"Use language that would disappoint my dearly-departed mother."

"Sorry for your loss."

"No loss. She just departed for her home in Baton Rouge today."

"Oh," I said.

"So will they let me into the opera like this?" I said to Larry to change the subject.

"Aren't going to the opera," he said.

"You didn't tell him?" said Tiffany.

"No. Don't you tell him either."

Tiffany's back straightened and I thought she was either going to tell me where we were going or tell Larry where he should go, but she just said, "You should have told him."

The route was familiar. As we turned onto the short side street that held Larry's gallery and not much else, I sighed and looked at Larry.

"I'm not going to give a speech tonight, Larry," I said.

"Don't have to."

"This isn't a setup, a little impromptu press conference where I'm supposed to stand up and tell a charming story about Marta? Sell a couple of paintings while I'm at it?"

"I'm doing the talking tonight."

We pulled up in front of the gallery. I looked up and saw a forty-foot banner, black in the middle and framed by the colors of Marta's palette. In the center were the words, "Marta, Farewell."

I looked back at Larry. He brushed past me and got out.

Tiffany patted me on the hand. "I'll take care of you, sugar."

Tiffany and I followed ten feet behind Larry. There was a crowd in the front room, obviously prepped and waiting for us. Larry jumped up on a small platform and all the eyes turned to him. I leaned on a wall at the back of the crowd.

"Friends," said Larry. He swept the crowd from one side to the other with a big salesman smile.

"We are here to celebrate, not to mourn. Six months ago, a light went out in the heavens. An angry, blazing star that turned all of our heads and made us all look up and see the sky in a way we had never seen, was extinguished. Because of the circumstances, we've never had a ceremony to pause, to celebrate, to thank Marta . . ." he paused and fixed me with a look.

". . . and to say goodbye one final time."

I turned to Tiffany.

She shrugged. "I told him to tell you."

I drifted away while Larry went on. The front room had pictures of Marta through the years. I walked around, following Marta's life. An opening here, a picture from an interview there. Our wedding picture.

I looked back at the crowd and couldn't find one true friend, not of mine or Marta's. Art—the act of creation and the connection to an audience—is all about authenticity and an unshakeable dedication to a vision that may never be shared or understood. Moneyed art is all about pretense and a carefully-constructed social consensus of greatness. Even if Marta had been dead, her soul wouldn't be here tonight.

I looked back at the wedding picture. It was only ten years old, but I felt like it should be sepia-toned and fraying. I had looked so young at twenty-five and now I felt so old at thirty-five. Marta was laughing a big wide-opened-mouth laugh and hurling a slice of wedding cake at the photographer. I stood just behind her shoulder patiently waiting for her to follow directions and feed me a slice of cake. I was smiling and slightly in shadow. It had been a comfortable place to be.

Tiffany touched my arm.

"What was it like," she said, "to be in love like that?"

"Heaven," I said. Thought another minute and said, "Hell, sometimes. You know the line, 'for better or worse'? It's what you sign up for."

I studied her face while she thought.

"You must know about that," I said.

"No."

"You don't seem that naïve."

"No," she laughed, but the laugh was sad. "Just never had that."

I looked at Tiffany a long time.

"Larry doesn't deserve you."

She thought a long time and gave the same laugh again.

"Too-pretty girls and too-rich men rarely get what they deserve." We stood in silence for a few seconds. "Or maybe we do," she said.

Larry was waving her over. She sighed and went to him.

I got a drink and a plate of hors d'oeuvres to keep myself busy. The plate was almost empty when Larry caught me.

"C'mon back," he said. He led me into his office. On his desk sat a dusty bottle of wine, with the cork and two glasses sitting beside it.

"Bought this at auction from that mutual fund billionaire who went to jail for running a Ponzi scheme."

"Which one?"

Larry laughed. "Yeah." He poured two glasses and passed me one.

"Here's to you." He raised his glass. "To battles fought and won, and to a time of peace. Tonight was all about you, my friend."

I wasn't ready to raise my glass. "I thought it was all about selling those paintings of Marta's you brought out tonight, the ones that you said weren't good enough to sell a year ago."

"That, too." He started to take a sip, but had something to say. He sat the glass down.

"Marta's gone," he said.

"You don't know that."

"I do. So do you, deep down inside. And you know that it's time you moved on."

"Her body's never been found. She could still be out there. And there are some strange things happening." I told him about the break-in and the Leongolian. He went into lawyer-mode, sat with his fingers together in a steeple, nodding his head and listening without interrupting.

"Let me handle that. I'll see what I can find out. You need to move on."

"She could still be out there."

Larry shrugged. "Could be. I pray that she is. But if she is, she's moved on. Or forgotten about both of us. Anyway, she's not coming back."

"I'm not like you, Larry. One Sheila-Tiffany walks out the door, you grab the next one."

He didn't flinch. "Yeah, I tried that, 'for-better-or-worse' thing a couple of times. Still writing the checks for it. But, you know, Paul, there's another part to that vow: 'till death do us part.' Whether Marta's alive somewhere or not, she's died to this life and moved on. You need to, too."

I stared into my glass.

Larry leaned forward. "Look, I didn't know you very well until this last year. You were always the good-natured patsy who put up with Marta's shenanigans. Some of us never understood why you did."

"Some of her shenanigans were good things to put up with," I said. "I remember the day I came back from the river and found a homeless family living in our house."

"Yeah," said Larry. "Remember that, too. Remember Marta demanding that I give them all jobs. Course, back then, her paintings weren't selling and it was easy for me to say no."

I said, "That's my point: I couldn't say no. Not then; not now. If I could have said no to Marta back then, I would have thrown the Wadleys out of the house. I couldn't. I bitched when Marta made me fix up an old house for them, bitched about how they dirtied up our house. I bitched about everything, but because I couldn't say no, that family is on its feet, and I've got a lot of great memories. It's something I'm proud of that I never would have done without Marta's passion in my life."

Larry dropped his voice. "There were some bad memories, too, my friend."

"Yes," I said. "Yes. There were."

"Marta would get off on some impossible lunatic cause, kick up a lot of dust, and expect you to fix things."

"Yeah. I griped about it, but I enjoyed fixing things."

"Some things you couldn't fix."

He paused and I didn't answer.

"Jail," he said.

I didn't answer.

"Drugs."

I didn't answer. He started to say something else.

"Drop it," I said. "I see where you're going. And you're right, Marta made life hell sometimes. But she gave my life passion."

Larry swirled his glass.

"Maybe it's time," he said. "To make your own passion. Stop hanging around the gallery, mooning over Marta's paintings. Stop giving lectures and interviews about Marta. Move on."

"That might cost you money," I said.

"Imagine," he looked up with a fake noble pose. "Me choosing friendship over money."

He looked at me and he could tell I was thinking about what he said.

"All right," he said. "Small steps. One week. One week, with no Marta. No looking at her paintings, no fixing her messes, nothing. Just peace and quiet and moving on with your own life."

I looked at Larry a long time before I raised my glass.

"I'll drink to that."

CHAPTER 15

Saturday morning, I paddled in straight lines toward places I'd never been. I tied up at a dock I had never noticed, walked up the street to a bakery I'd never seen and bought bagels to take back to the shop.

I felt expanded. I told myself that I was just humoring Larry; give myself one Marta-less week to placate him. But there was more. I went to the store that night and bought hamburger meat even though Marta hated beef. Invited my neighbor over and we grilled burgers and drank beer. He peeked up at Marta's window once, out of habit, afraid of a tirade exploding from the window. We laughed at that, then sat on the front porch and picked at songs and talked football until the beer was gone. When he left and I was cleaning the grill, I looked up at Marta's window and realized I had been looking at that window for too long, waiting for the excitement and adventure in my life to come from it. Larry was right. I needed my own life.

Monday morning, I was on my computer charting a week-long trip on a California river I had never seen. The phone rang.

"Hey," said Larry.

"Hey," I said after the pause. I'd never heard Larry give a one-word greeting before. Usually, he was halfway through a four-act sales pitch before he would take his first breath.

"I need you to come down here."

"What, we're going to have a surprise memorial at your law

office, too? C'mon, Larry, I got things to do. That speech you gave me worked; I'm making plans."

"Yeah."

There was a long pause.

"No, really, Paul, I need you down here, soon as you can get here."

I hopped into The Beast and maneuvered it through Portland traffic to Larry's office on Hawthorne. Larry's assistant Gwen gave me a worried smile and waved me to the conference room. I opened the door and saw the river, broad and busy, weaving in and out of the Portland skyline in the glass wall behind the table. At the table next to Larry sat a tiny, shriveled-up gray-suited man hunched over some papers.

I stepped into the room and let the door close behind me. Larry gave an irritated wave at something behind the door. I turned and saw Detective Ahlstrom standing behind me.

Ahlstrom's face lit up with a crooked grimace that tried to be a smile. He grabbed my hand and pumped it like I was a best friend that he hadn't seen in years. I let my arm go limp and he just kept shaking and grinning. I slowly realized that, in his strange and lonely mind, I might be his best friend—and a target.

"Got you that time, didn't I?" He pulled away, cocked his hand like a gun and gave me two quick shots. "Been hiding back there for five minutes, waiting to surprise you." He clapped me on the shoulder. "Good to see you. When we going canoeing again?"

I realized my mouth was hanging open and I closed it.

"Kayaking," I said. "Next time there's a missing person who happens to be my wife, I'll call you. Or not."

Ahlstrom laughed like it was the funniest thing he'd heard. Larry motioned me to the seat next to him. Ahlstrom started to sit next to me, still with the grin on his face like he had a joke to tell his old friend.

Larry shook his head. "Detective, I'd like you to sit on the other side of the table. Or maybe someplace in Canada." Ahlstrom went around the table and sat down.

The tiny man looked off into empty space and spoke with no emotion. "I've requested that Detective Ahlstrom sit in on this meeting."

"That's why he gets to stay," said Larry. "As long as he keeps his mouth shut."

Ahlstrom was still grinning. He jerked his chin at the little man. "Yeah, Jenkins here called down to the station to ask about the case, they patched him through to me, I told him I wouldn't miss this for the world."

"Yeah, well, you're an observer," said Larry. "That's all."

"So let's observe."

Larry shook his head. "Mr. Jenkins, the floor is yours."

Jenkins looked off in space again. His mouth moved but nothing else even seemed alive.

"I represent the Northern California Insurance Corporation. Some time back, an agent of ours filed a new policy, but did not correctly complete the procedure to enter it into our system. This has, unfortunately, resulted in the policy being misplaced for six months. The Northern California Insurance Corporation apologizes for any inconvenience this delay may have brought to any party or parties.

"I have this day delivered a copy of said policy to Mr. Larry Maldeve here as representative of the estate of Ms. Marta Strauss-McClaron."

Larry cut him off and looked at me.

"Paul, two days before her disappearance, Marta took out a life insurance policy for five million dollars, payable to you."

My mouth dropped open but Ahlstrom put his hand up in a

high five for me to slap. I ignored him and Larry gave him a dirty look.

"Paul, do you know anything about this?"

Everyone looked at me. "No. We had a policy for a hundred thousand that you knew about. We haven't filed it until things are . . . resolved."

Jenkins nodded, "There are a number of technicalities and difficulties with this policy as well."

Ahlstrom laughed. "I bet. Here, let me see that." He reached over and snatched the paper from Jenkins and studied it.

Larry said, "Detective, please return the application."

"In a minute. Let me see this signature." He pulled a sheet out of his coat pocket and laid it next to the application. "See, if it looks like her signature, that means she's in on it, and that makes it fraud. If he forged the signature, well, that makes it murder." He studied the signature and looked up at me with a bright smile. "Good news, pal. Her signature. Looks like fraud instead of murder."

Larry snatched the paper back. "Or any number of other things."

"That's great news," said Ahlstrom. "When I solve this, you're looking at—what—twenty years, maybe less. Don't know, never worked insurance fraud before. But murder, well, you know, you'd be paddling your kayak in the prison yard till you rot."

"Look, you're an observer. Observe in silence or leave. Mr. Jenkins and Mr. McClaron and I have a lot to talk about."

Ahlstrom nodded. The music from *Shaft* filled the room. Ahlstrom fished a phone out of his pocket and ignored the rest of us.

"Yeah? I'm working here," he yelled into the phone.

He paused.

"Well, get somebody else to work that. I got a case already."

Longer pause.

"Well, fire me then."

He hung up.

Larry said, "I sincerely hope that was the chief of police."

"Nah, just my lieutenant."

"Good for him or her," said Larry. "I've warned you before to keep quiet. Now I'd like you to leave."

Ahlstrom looked at me for a long time. "He don't want me to leave."

I didn't say anything.

"I sympathize with you, pal," he said. "Maybe even admire you for whatever the hell you've done, even though I'm going to put you away for it. But look around this table, even look around the whole damned city. You and I are the only ones that want to find Marta. Ain't that what you want?"

He stared at me a long time with his awkward grin.

"I'm your only hope."

CHAPTER 16

"You don't need to listen to Ahlstrom," said Larry.

We were walking down Hawthorne Boulevard. Larry was angry and walking fast, dodging people on the sidewalk and talking back over his shoulder.

"He's an asshole," he said.

"King of them all, as far as that goes," I said. "But he still might be right."

I walked around the side of the Bread and Ink Café to the bright-blue Waffle Window cut into the side of the building. Took a place in line behind a couple of teenagers in tie-dyed robes and a young mother trying to keep three young kids straight while she ordered at the window. Looked back and saw Larry motioning to me at the door of the café.

"Full price today?" I said.

"Need to get somewhere to talk privately," he said. "I'll charge it to you anyhow."

"Should have guessed."

Bread and Ink Café is a good, moderately upscale café. The people sitting at the tables wore suits and expensive dresses. But—in true Portland fashion—the owner wanted to make sure everybody had access to his food. So you could either sit in the café, have a waiter bring your order, and pay a café price, or if you just wanted food, rather than atmosphere, you could order at the Waffle Window outside, pay about half price, get a waffle on a paper plate, and take it to either a picnic table outside or a long rough table inside with benches. Usually, we sat outside.

"We'll have a Banana Rumba Waffle and a Bacon-Brie-Basil Waffle. Two coffees," said Larry to our waiter.

"No," I said. "Want something different today. Change the Bacon-Brie-Basil to a Whole Farm."

"Never seen you get anything but Three B's," said Larry.

"I am," I said, "spreading my wings. Exploring new worlds. Reinventing the Paul McClaron franchise."

"Spinning a new line of bullshit," said Larry.

"That, too."

The mother from the line was trying to herd her kids into place around the long table inside, while juggling a couple of paper plates of waffles. Wasn't having much luck. I stood up to go help.

A tall man balancing his own paper plate beat me to it. He set his plate on the table, took the plates from the mother and helped them get settled. He was a big man: dark-skinned and apparently Native American, with a navy-blue Armani suit and a bolo tie with a turquoise-and-silver clasp, and his sleek black hair pulled back in a ponytail. He had the sad-eyed, deeply-lined look of the chiefs from the old photographs, coupled with the clean-scrubbed confidence of the modern rich and elite. The mother smiled shyly and thanked him as he sat down next to them, his clothes standing out at the half-price table the same way his look stood out from the rest of us.

I wished that I had moved faster; helped the mother before he had, earned the smile for helping her. Maybe I was listening too much to Rue. Soon, I'd be hearing the universe in my ear.

I sat back down.

"So," said Larry. "You accept that Ahlstrom's just trying to get under your skin?"

"Always," I said.

"He's not your friend."

"No."

"Don't let him get you hooked into chasing after Marta."

I couldn't think of anything to say. I looked over at the Native American. I had decided I needed to make more friends; expand my circle. He had been glancing over at me. I smiled at him. He looked away and pretended not to notice. Clearly, my social skills need work.

"You need to let me handle this," said Larry. "This could get nasty. With this much money, the insurance company will hire investigators. Their lawyers will look for ways out."

Larry scanned the room, trying to look bored.

"Course, any publicity now will help sell paintings."

Except the truth, I thought. The laughable artist who faked her death.

"Look, I don't care, Larry," I said. "I don't need the money. The shop's doing OK. Marta's paintings are selling. I've got money. Not five million dollars, but all I need. Let's just drop it."

Our food arrived. My waffle was piled with bacon, mushrooms, spinach, roasted bell peppers, chevre cheese and tomatoes. I looked at it and assumed I was going to be napping this afternoon.

"Too late to drop it," said Larry. "Turn it down now, and you'll just look guilty. Your buddy Ahlstrom will get a bunch of assistants to nail you. And he will nail you, eventually, for something."

I was several bites in when I noticed Larry hadn't started eating.

"Any idea why Marta bought five million dollars worth of insurance just before an accident?"

I stopped eating and looked at him. He hadn't picked up his fork. His hands were pressed together like a steeple in his lawyer-listening pose.

"You know Marta." I looked away. "Just one of those things Marta did on a whim."

"Yeah," he said. "Sounds like Marta's kind of wild and crazy whim, run out and pick up a bagel and a five-million-dollar insurance policy. Probably bought some sensible shoes while she was at it."

"Maybe she loved me," I said. "Maybe she wants me to have the money. Maybe she wants me to hold on to the money for both of us because she's coming back. Larry, I don't know. I'm as confused as you are."

He waited on me to go on, but I just took a bite and kept chewing, trying to look at him with no expression on my face. He looked at me a long time.

"You were the one that was sure this was an accident," he said. I kept chewing. Wished there was a mirror behind Larry so I could see what my face looked like.

"Yeah, you're right," I said.

"Paul, there's something you're not telling me," he said. Another long pause.

"You need to tell your lawyer everything."

But you can't tell your wife's agent everything.

CHAPTER 17

I left The Beast parked at Larry's office and walked around. I wasn't sure if I was walking home or just walking around. Not sure if it mattered. I needed to talk and I had no one to talk to so I wandered the streets and muttered to myself like the other street people. I was stopped in the middle of the sidewalk, people flowing around me while I argued with Marta, when a smiling man shoved a dollar in my hand and said "Bless you" as he walked by.

I stopped talking to Marta in mid-sentence, looked at the bill in my hand. Looked down at the sawdust covering my work clothes and understood. In my line of sight behind the bill, out of focus, a real panhandler sat on the curb with a cardboard sign, "War veteran." I shifted my focus, saw the vacant eyes and the dirty clothes that I usually politely stepped around. Wondered if I was looking at an exaggerated version of myself, the old veteran unable to move on from memories and obligations, unable to move into a future without the things he had once taken for granted. Except that he had reasons and I just had excuses.

I shoved the dollar into his shirt and walked on, walking too fast for my mind to wander.

I heard a crowd laughing in a pocket park and went over to watch a band of street performers. I stopped at the back of the crowd, close enough to hear the words but only able to see the heads of the men in the troupe over the crowd. Dressed in makeshift costumes, they were doing a bawdy parody of Shakespeare with little acrobatic stunts punctuating the punch lines, all focused on a tall man with manic energy and a jester's cap. The jester's head, floating above the crowd, turned to a guy with the head of Darth Vader.

"Knock knock," he said.

"Who's there?"

"Noah."

"Noah who?"

"Noah's the winter of our discontent."

A drum somewhere gave a rim shot, and one of the acrobats jumped onto Darth Vader's shoulders and did a swan dive into the crowd.

The jokes got worse but the energy was good. Finally, the jester looked right at me and deadpanned, "To be or not to be, that is a question?"

Several of the men in the troupe threw a woman in tights and a harlequin top high into the air. She floated in the air like she was lying on her side, one hand holding her head like she was resting on a couch.

It was Rue, floating in mid-air, winking at me before she fell out of the sky. I made my way through the crowd and found her thanking people as they dropped money into an open guitar case. A little girl dropped a dime into the case, Rue gave her a big hug and the girl skipped away grinning like she had won a prize.

"So this is your real job?" I said.

"Everything's my real job."

"Does your real job ever let you take a dinner break?"

"Sure," she said. "Give me a minute."

The money was divided up. She took a wad of bills from the jester without counting them.

"Now," she said, "if we can find a true vegan restaurant. Or

97

Thai. I'm not that strict."

I laughed. "This is Portland. Easier for you to find vegan than for me to find a hamburger."

She scrunched her nose at me and took off down the street. I hurried to catch up. I thought she was looking for a place to eat, but she was bouncing from one street person to the next, peeling bills off as she went, folding the bills into their hands and saying "Thank you" to each of them. We passed a couple of restaurants before the money was gone.

"I take it the rich capitalist gets to buy dinner," I said, when she handed out the last dollar. It sounded funnier in my head than it did when I actually said it, but she laughed anyway.

"If the rich capitalist wants to eat he pays for his dinner." She ducked into a little Indian place. "I pay my own way."

We ordered. Rue stopped chattering, folded her hands, and sat there with her enigmatic smile. I waited for her to say something. The restaurant spun around us: waiters skipping past like dancers in a ballet, voices rising and falling like music. We, however, were as still as statues. She was good at it. I was not.

"Cat got your tongue?" I said. It was the cleverest thing I could think of.

"You," she said, nothing but her mouth moving, "have something you want to say to me."

"No I don't."

She nodded. "You have a hole in your soul. You need to talk."

"Maybe. Sometimes, though, you can't talk about what you need to talk about."

"Sometimes," she said, "we have to talk around the edges of things, just ease into what's important."

"Not if you have promises and obligations, things you can't say because they would affect other people."

"But you need someone to listen, even when you can't talk."

She put her hand on mine and her smile became warm and sexy. At least to me. It felt too good to me, and I jerked my hand back.

She laughed. "Am I really that scary?"

She withdrew her hand.

"I'm a very good listener, Paul. Got a couple of fancy degrees to prove it, from big colleges. Even spent a couple of years working as a counselor."

"So you used to be in the real world. What happened?"

"Talk therapy seemed too much and too little at the same time, and it took too much time and changed people too little. One day, I had a woman referred to me by the drug court. I could see that she was so close to breaking through, and I could see that if she left my office and went back to the halfway house and back to the same old friends, she was going to use again and she would be back in her old life. So I took her home, cleaned her up. Coached her until she found a job and got her own place. Very unprofessional. Therapists aren't supposed to get that close. Scandalized the therapeutic community. My boyfriend—my last boyfriend, I might add, last boyfriend I will ever have—couldn't take my turning our lives upside down and ran away screaming and demanding. I decided that day not to take orders from anybody but the universe, and the universe told me that there were only two ways to help any human being: either you give a little unexpected gesture—a buck to a street person, a pat on a child's head—or you roll up your hands and give everything you've got to someone, even if it's only for a little while. Anything else is bullshit."

"The universe lets you use bad words like that?"

"You think," she said, "the universe is all sweetness and light?"

"No," I said slowly. "I do not. Right now it makes no sense to me at all."

"What do you want it to be?"

"Clean waters, clear paths," I thought. "Simple."

Rue laughed. "Good luck with that."

"You could be right. That's not the universe I'm finding now. Right now, I'm starting to feel like I want to go forward, but your universe keeps pulling me back. You talk to the universe on a regular basis. Ever think maybe there's more than one universe; maybe I'm torn between two of them?"

"No. There's only one. Listen, she'll give you what you need and tell you what to do with it, if you just listen."

The waiter set our food down.

"See?" said Rue. She picked up her plate. "A gift from the universe."

"So what do you do," I said, "when you need to talk and you can't talk?"

"You act," she said. "Take what the universe puts in front of you, and act on it the best way you know how." She picked up a fork and took a bite of tofu in hot sauce. "Be grateful first, and the universe will reward you."

So we sat there and rewarded ourselves silently for a while. I was grateful for the food, grateful for the silence. Grateful to have the questions in my head silenced for a few minutes by spices and flavor. Funny, simply feeling grateful helped to clear my head. When our plates were empty, she flicked the smallest smile at our waiter and he came running over.

"Pay the man for your dinner." She stood up and handed the waiter a handful of wadded-up bills.

I took the bill from him, figured how much I owed, calculated a twenty-per-cent tip, and paid. Rue was already walking to the door.

"Where are we going?" I said.

"Therapy."

We stepped out to the street.

"Right or left?" she said.

"I don't know. My car's back that way, but I don't know . . ."

"No," she said. "I want you to find a way to listen to yourself. We're going to play a game called, 'Follow the Universe.' Hold your arm straight up."

"I don't get it," I said.

"Reach your arm straight up high, like you're trying to grab a piece of the sky."

I did. Felt foolish standing in the street with my arm straight up.

"Grab the sky. Now, with the sky in your hand, let your arm go limp and fall."

I did.

"OK, did it fall to the left or the right?"

"A little to the right, I guess."

"We go right."

I tried it a couple of times, standing there in the middle of the street. I was surprised that I wasn't embarrassed anymore, but Rue made things that had felt weird feel good.

"It's not random," I said. "It's going to fall to the left most times. I think my subconscious mind made it fall to the right, not the universe."

"You say subconscious mind, I say universe. Not supposed to be random. Learn to make decisions, press forward, listen to yourself, even if your conscious mind doesn't want to."

She turned and marched right. There was a guy passed out on the sidewalk. She stopped in front of him.

"You or me?"

I held up my arm and it fell toward her.

"You," I said. I was getting the hang of this. Random turns, random choices on who took action.

Rue took out a dollar and shoved it in the guy's pocket. We marched on, came to an intersection.

"Left or . . ."

"Got it." I held up my hand and let it drop. "Left. Cross the street."

On the other side, I said "Left" and we walked down the street facing the restaurant we had come out of. There was a guy slumped against a wall facing the restaurant.

"Me," I said.

I took out a five and looked down at a pair of navy blue Armani suit pants. Looked into the face of the Native American from lunch. His eyes were closed and he was making snoring noises. His jacket was rolled up and tucked behind him and his pants were shoved into the top of his socks to look sloppy, but it was the same guy in the same suit. When I shoved the bill in his pocket, I could see that one eye wasn't quite closed.

Rue was already walking. I caught up.

"I know that guy," I said.

"We are all connected." She didn't slow down.

"No, I mean . . ." I turned back to look at him. He was on his feet, hurrying away from us.

"Hey," I yelled. He looked back at me and ducked down an alley.

"Hey," I yelled again and took off after him.

CHAPTER 18

I chased the man for answers and found myself in a blind alley that was empty, mere seconds behind the man in Armani, and looked at three brick walls stretching to the sky and nothing else but random trash.

Rue ran up beside me.

"What is wrong with you?"

"That man—he ran in here after he saw us."

"So?"

"I saw this guy at lunch, now I saw him again."

"Ah, so you were chasing him because he ate lunch. That makes sense."

"He's following me."

"You're sure about this?"

"His clothes. At lunch he was dressed up, Armani suit. Now he's a street person."

"He did have nice pants."

"See?"

"Ok, so why's he following you?"

I stood there and didn't say anything.

"I get it," said Rue. "Another one of those things you want to talk about but can't talk about."

"You got it. Maybe. But we don't have him. He went in here and disappeared."

"Disappeared?" She frowned at me. "And people say I'm a flake."

"All right." I waved at the empty alley. "Didn't go left. Didn't go right."

She studied the alley.

"The universe says he went up."

"Flew away on a cloud?"

She made a face and pointed at a set of iron rungs in the back corner.

"Oh," I said.

"C'mon." Rue turned around and took off running. I caught up.

"If he went up on the roof there; he's got to come down, probably one street over."

We turned one corner; turned the next.

"There," said Ruc. He was ahead of us.

"Wait," I yelled. "We just want to talk."

Unimpressed, he started running. I caught up and grabbed one shoulder. He spun, pushed me away, and dashed across the street, cars honking.

Rue hurdled onto the hood of a parked car, bounced from there to the hood of a car in traffic, from there to the roof of a pickup truck going the other way. Gathered herself and flew off the truck at the running man.

She hit his trailing shoulder and they both went down in a pile. He bounced up first and threw her away like a toy. She landed feet first and came at him. Grabbed an arm, spun him around and pushed him into a brick wall.

"Assume the position," she said. She was breathing hard but her voice was flat and calm.

"You a cop?" he said.

"C'mon." She kicked his feet apart. "Spread 'em."

I caught up.

"You used to be a cop, too?" I said.

She said nothing until she had both feet apart and his face in the wall.

"No," she finally said once he was under control. "Picked that up watching TV.

"Here," she said. "You take him for a minute and let me check my knee."

I locked my hands on his biceps, not sure of what to do. Turned him around so I could face him. I turned loose and shook my finger in his face.

"Don't you dare move," I said, in my sternest voice.

He looked over my shoulder at something and his mouth opened in terror at what he saw. I turned and saw nothing but cars in the street. I turned back just in time to see a fist that looked like a runaway planet crash into my face.

I woke up with the same Samoan doctor leaning over me, back in the emergency room.

"We don't give any kind of two-for-one specials, sir," he said, in a surprisingly high voice. "You don't need to come back again."

"Mr. McClaron needs to go home," said Rue's voice behind him. "Watch some TV, and learn from it."

CHAPTER 19

I was in the shop the next day. My head hurt, but I was starting to think that feeling bad was my new normal. I looked up at the door and I was sure of it.

Ahlstrom came in with a big grin. Pulled a paddle from a rack on the wall and beat the air furiously with it.

"Man, I miss the water," he said. He knocked over a display rack and glared at it like it was the rack's fault. I pointed to the wall and he hung the paddle back up and skipped over to me.

"What are you doing tonight, partner?" he said.

"Staying out of jail. Staying away from you."

"Heh heh heh." He reached in his coat and pulled out a menu from a low-rent downtown steakhouse known for its gristle and brown salads. Slapped it down on the counter and I winced from the noise.

"Be there," he said. "Seven o'clock."

"I wouldn't be there if I were dead. What did you do, steal one of their menus?"

"Like an invitation."

"You're a cop. You stole one of their menus rather than make your own invitation?"

"I figured I was due." He pulled himself close and grinned. "I've rented the place."

"Must have set you back a whole dollar."

"Naw, didn't cost anything." He hesitated. "Didn't really rent the whole place."

"So you reserved a table?"

"Big table. You'll see."

"Won't see. Won't be there. At seven o'clock tonight I'll be anywhere but there. If I get the urge to go there, I'll just go home and throw up, save myself the middle step of eating their lousy food and listening to your lousy insults."

"Heh heh heh. Boy, I love this witty banter you and me have. No, you'll be there. There's an important announcement there, one you want to hear."

"Just tell me here. Better yet, tell my lawyer and leave me out of this."

He waggled his finger back and forth in front of me.

"Not going to be that easy. See, now I've created a mystery for you. You'll be there."

"No way."

He turned and walked to the door. Spun around with his hands out like two guns.

"Seven o'clock. Be there." He jabbed the guns at me. "Or be square."

I should have picked square. Seven-fifteen, and I was standing on the sidewalk outside of the restaurant, pacing, telling myself I was trying to decide, but I knew the decision had already been made. At least I had eaten before I came down.

I stepped inside and my eyes slowly adjusted to the dark, like a movie scene slowly coming up in muted grays and browns. A couple of families here to take advantage of the all-you-can-eat buffet. Drunk couple in the corner. A few bored waiters. And there in the corner sat a man at a long, empty table with his head down, three empty beer bottles on the table in front of him. Ahlstrom.

I walked over and stood looking down at him. A waiter appeared at my elbow.

"Friend?" he said.

"No. How long has he been like this?"

"Came in at ten till seven. Raised hell with the manager because the table wasn't big enough. Paced around, practicing smiles and a speech until seven. The smile started to droop. At seven-oh-five, he said, 'They're not coming.' Ordered three beers, chugged them while he was crying. And here we are." He waved at Ahlstrom. "You going to take him home?"

"No." I pulled up a chair and sat down.

"Can I get you anything, sir?"

I looked at the wilted and dirty food on the buffet. "How about a bottle of beer, unopened, and a bag of chips, also unopened."

"Excellent choice." He walked away.

I poked Ahlstrom.

"Leave me alone," he said. Muffled and slurred, it sounded more like "leb bone" but I got the idea.

"C'mon," I said. "Shake off this big drunk of yours and talk to me."

He raised his head. I was surprised to see how red his eyes were from three beers. Realized that crying would do that to your eyes, too.

"Thirty-seven years," he said. He swept his arm at the table. "See what it gets you."

He paused like I was supposed to understand that.

"Not a one of them."

Another pause.

"Not my first partner."

Another pause.

"Even after I was there for him after his wife left him. Course she left him 'cause she thought we—my partner and I—were having an affair. Thought I was a faggot. I ain't no faggot. Faggots go to hell. I went to her, tried to explain it to her, but I guess it all came out wrong and she left him after that. He blamed me."

Another pause.

"Still, he ought to be here. Your partner ought to be here. Lieutenant ought to be here, too. Said today was the happiest day of his life. Promised me he would celebrate tonight."

He looked at me. "You see the Lieutenant here? Do you?"

"No," I said. "Look, Ahlstrom, what are you saying? Why are these guys supposed to be here?"

"My goddamned retirement." He screamed. I looked around. Nobody was even looking at us. Deranged screams must be a daily special here.

"Look at this." He waved a framed citation at me. I took it away. "Captain gave it to me today." He sat there silently. "I told him I was going to retire. He smiled, reached in his drawer, pulled out some papers and said, 'I've been keeping these for you.' Showed me where to sign and date them. I asked him how much notice he needed. He said, 'None. You can leave now.' I asked him, 'Don't I get a plaque or a watch or something?' He said, 'Sure.' Printed this up on his computer, took one of his awards off the wall, used the frame to make me this."

I looked at the citation. It just said, "Martin Alstrom is retired from the Portland Police Department as of today." No date. "Ahlstrom" was misspelled.

"Very nice." I handed it back to Ahlstrom.

"I'll show them," he said. Grinned at me and said, "We'll show them."

I waited.

"Got a new job," he finally said.

"Going to get rich, you and me," he said.

I waited some more.

"Took a job with that insurance company, the one that you and your wife are trying to fleece for five million dollars. See, I'm now an investigator for them. Why I retired. I prove your wife is alive, and they pay me ten percent of the five million that I've saved them."

He put his face in mine. "Five hundred thousand dollars."

"Congratulations."

He shook his head.

"Not just me getting rich here, partner."

He smiled like I was supposed to know what that meant. It occurred to me that I might be rich if I knew half the things other people thought I knew, or if I could talk to them about what I did know.

"One hundred thousand dollars." He breathed so much beer into my face that I thought he might sober up.

"That's for you," he said. "Figure, I give you a hundred thousand. You tell me where Marta is, and I collect five hundred thousand." He leaned back. "Everybody wins."

"Course, I go to jail," I said.

"Well, of course," he said. "But that's going to happen anyway. You've got your own personal cop—ex-cop—watching you twenty-four seven until I get my money."

I paid for his beers and put him in a taxi.

CHAPTER 20

I got my truck and drove home, determined to curl up with a Western where everything was clear and the cowboys always won.

I parked in the garage and walked around to the front door. Hesitated a minute with the key in the lock, not sure what I would find on the other side. Smiled at how paranoid I was becoming. I was a quiet man on a quiet street in a quiet town. It had been days since my house had been ransacked.

Nevertheless, I locked the door behind me after I went in. Stood there silently, listening for any sound. Heard nothing, but turned on all the lights and checked all the closets. Went through the house holding a kitchen knife and checked everything until I was sure I was better off holding a beer than a knife. I took my beer into the living room, settled into the couch and turned on the Western channel.

A deep voice said, "Kind of rude, don't you think?"

I jumped, spilled my beer, and looked. Sitting in the corner chair was the Native American in the blue Armani suit. He hadn't been there a minute ago.

"I mean," he said, "you have an Indian houseguest, so you figure he wants to watch other Indians—probably being played by a European actor like yourself—being portrayed as a race of simpletons, biding their time waiting for some heroic Europeans to come slaughter them?"

I didn't know what to say. "I thought you preferred to be

called Native Americans?"

He smiled a big, toothy, fake smile designed to make me uncomfortable.

"I'll go along with 'Native Americans' when it's a real badge of honor, when I can turn on a Sunday morning political talk show and see the host say, 'Now we'll see what the Native Americans think,' and have everyone wait breathlessly while the *real* Americans weigh in. Till then—as long as 'Native American' is just a polite way to pretty up history and pretend it never happened—I'll stick with 'Indian.' Reminds me of how ignorant you guys are about us."

"Oh," I said, still not sure how to play this. It was my first time being threatened. If that's what was happening.

"Well," I said. "Would you like to watch something else?"

Big toothy smile. "I'd like to watch you squirm."

Answered the question about being threatened.

"Or you can just give me my five million dollars and you can go back to your racist TV program."

I was surprised. "How do you know about the five million dollars?"

Now he was surprised. "So you admit that you've got it?"

"I don't have it. You must know that."

We looked at each other for a long time. He stood up and sighed.

"For a minute there," he said. "I thought this one was going to be easy."

He reached back for a coil of rope he had been sitting on and motioned me to a wooden rocking chair. I stood up, too. He was big, but I was bigger.

"You got a gun?" I said.

"I don't need a gun. Got a knife."

He reached back and pulled out a long, shining knife. I shifted to one side and reached for a lamp to block him. He was faster, caught my arm and wrenched it behind me with no apparent effort on his part. A searing pain ripped out of my shoulder but I kept quiet.

He brought his face up to the side of mine. "This tells me," he said, "how much pain you can take before I can trust what you say." Gave one little jerk and I was ready to say anything.

He pushed me over to the rocking chair. I tried to sit down.

"No," he said. "Bring it in the kitchen, in the back part of the house."

I dragged the chair with my free hand while he shoved me and the chair into the kitchen. Thought about trying to hit him with the chair, but he stayed behind me and I could feel the knife in my back.

"Over there," he said, "facing the stove."

He put me in the chair and tied my forearms to the chair's arms. He pulled up a kitchen chair next to the stove and faced me. I looked out the window and hoped Ahlstrom was right about watching me, but there was no one there.

"Now," he said, "you can give me the money, and I'll be out of your hair. If you don't, being an Indian, I might just take your hair. It is, I assure you, a painful process."

"What money?"

"My five million. I don't want any more. I am not a thief."

"I don't know what you're talking about."

"You knew about it a minute ago."

"I don't have your five million. I don't know the five million you mean."

He smiled. "This is a first. I've never met a man who had so many piles of five million dollars lying around that he doesn't know which one we're talking about. I'll give you a hint: Four Winds Casino."

"The Native American—Indian casino on the coast? Wait a minute. There are several legitimate casinos, run by legitimate

113

tribes. Four Winds is the one run by the tribe that some people say is fake. You're part of them?"

He shrugged. "I'm Blackfoot. Came west because Oregon's a little more open-minded. My people back home are not too accepting of gay Indians. They thought I was great when I was the smart kid winning scholarships. Stopped putting my picture in the tribal paper once they realized my fascination with spears was more than symbolic. Heard a lot of jokes about dressing in feathers, how I wasn't supposed to save a horse, ride a cowboy . . ."

"Got it," I stopped him. "I heard a lot of jokes myself, growing up. I wasn't gay, but I was the big, clumsy kid. People can be cruel."

"You know it. So I went back East to school. Got tired of that when all the philosophy and psychology started to sound like a load of European American cultural propaganda. Took the job as a collector of bad debts for a group of casinos out here. Pays good, I get a lot of time for reading." He looked at me with a cold look. "Every time I have to break a leg or convince someone to pay a bill, I just think of the way the tough guys in the tribe used to pound on me."

"You seem too smart for this. You could make a living a lot of other ways. What about jail? Do this long enough, sooner or later you're going to wind up in jail."

He smiled a big toothy grin. "Prison, for me, seems like a big buffet."

I needed to change the subject or take a shower.

"I don't get it. I've never been to your casino."

"Your wife has."

"Marta?"

He leaned in and watched me closely for a reaction. "What? You got multiple wives, one for each stack of five million dollars? Yes, Marta—the wife who robbed the casino of five million dollars."

"Holy smoke," I said.

He leaned back and smiled. "See, that was a tell. Any man who's just found out his wife committed a multi-million dollar robbery; he's going to yell something like, 'Shit' or maybe worse. But 'Holy smoke?' Now that's about as fake as they come."

"No, really, that's just . . . Why would Marta do that? She didn't care that much for money. I always gave her everything she needed."

"Apparently not. There was something she needed she couldn't get from you."

I didn't have an answer to that. He leaned back and watched me.

"Look, people are always more complicated than anyone thinks, have needs that their loved ones would never guess at. Look at me."

I nodded, but I wasn't sure what I was agreeing to.

"I like talking to you," he said. "You seem like a decent man, trying to protect his wife. You take me for what I am. Not a lot of people I can talk to. But, fun as this is, we've got business to attend to, and I'd like to get on the road before morning."

He reached back and turned on one of the burners. A blue flame hissed to life.

"So you say you don't know where the money is?" He turned the knife back and forth in the flame.

"I swear I don't. Maybe Marta took it with her." He looked at me. "When . . . she . . . died." I finished.

He laughed. "We'd look in the casket, but I understand that there isn't one."

The blade glowed red in the flame.

"So you understand that I can't just take your word for this. Here's an old Indian trick: You put a knife in the fire and ask a man a question. Then you put the hot knife on his tongue. If he's telling the truth, the knife doesn't stick. If he's lying, well, it gets ugly and I have to clean the burned flesh off my knife.

"Even has a good scientific basis. If you aren't nervous, the saliva on your tongue will protect it. Course, if you're lying, your mouth dries up from the stress. Sssssssss."

"You're the one lying," I said. "That 'old Indian trick' came from a TV show called, *Law of the Plainsman,* back in the sixties."

He smiled. "Nevertheless, it works every time."

My mouth was getting dry.

"Have you ever," I said, "had a time when the knife didn't stick?"

"Never," he said, turning the knife in the flame.

"I've never found an honest man."

CHAPTER 21

I didn't trust the hot knife, I didn't trust the man, and I didn't want to be the first honest man in history to go through life with a fried tongue. I looked past him and tried to look terrified.

"You really think anyone is stupid enough to fall for that trick?" He laughed. "Oh yeah. I forgot. Sorry."

He studied the knife.

"Last chance."

"All right," I said. "Look in the oven."

"The oven? Are you nuts? What kind of an idiot puts five million dollars in cash in an oven where it can burn up?"

"Same kind that falls for the oldest trick in the book. Said it yourself. Stupid."

He looked at me and we both knew he didn't believe me and we both knew he had to look anyway. He edged over and opened the oven door without taking his eyes off me. But he had to turn, if only for a second, to look inside. In that second, I yanked up on the arms of the chair as hard as I could. He caught the end of the movement and looked back in time to see me sitting still in the chair.

"Didn't work, did it?" he said. "So much for finding an honest man."

But I had found what I was looking for: the back of the right arm was loose. I kept rocking side to side, trying to make it look like nervous energy. But it was a little looser every time.

He looked at me and put the blade back in the flame.

"Don't get nervous," he said. "Makes the knife stick worse."

The edge of the knife was glowing red, but he kept it in the flame.

"Look. Why don't you just tell me where the money is? All I want is the money."

"Would you believe me if I tell you that I've never heard of the money until today?"

He slowly shook his head.

"No," he said. "I wouldn't."

He turned off the burner. Slowly brought the knife over to my face.

"I'm sorry," he said.

I yanked hard on the arm and it ripped free. Stood up as the arm came loose and my fist and the arm of the chair connected with his face. He flew up into the air, crashed down on the floor and started to get up. I spun around with my left arm still tied to the chair and smashed the chair onto his head. It splintered into pieces and he didn't move.

"I'm not," I said.

I poked him with my toe and he didn't move. I kicked the knife to the other side of the room, peeled the chair away and reached into my tool drawer, pulled out a roll of electrician's tape and wrapped his hands together behind his back. Wasn't sure that was enough, so I kept going, wrapping around his legs and his arms and his neck until the tape ran out.

And then I stood there, wondering what to do next. I mean, what are you supposed to do with an unconscious man tied up on your kitchen floor?

In the movies, the marshal always throws a bucket of water on the guy to wake him up and make the guy confess. That seemed messy and somehow insulting to the Indian so I filled up a water glass instead. Drank half of it and then stood over him with the glass in one hand and a paper towel in the other. I poured a little on his forehead. Nothing happened, so I wiped it up to protect the floor. Dribbled a little on his eyes, and cleaned it up.

Pouring it up his nose worked. He sputtered to life. Once he stopped hacking and coughing, he said, "You didn't have to do that."

"You were going to fricassee my tongue. Seemed like I needed to do something."

"I wouldn't have done that. I've never actually done that. Seems like something a savage would do."

"But you do break legs when you have to?"

"Of course."

"Kill people?"

"Only once. Well, maybe twice."

"Over a lot less money than five million?"

He didn't answer.

"What's your name?"

"Call me Owl. Symbol of wisdom for the coast tribes."

"I've never had a wise man tied up on my kitchen floor with electrical tape before."

"We don't have a word for that."

"Probably not."

I pulled up a chair and sat down facing him.

"Owl—if I can call you that without laughing right now—I need to know what you know about Marta."

"Nothing."

"Jesus. Am I supposed to heat up the knife now, make you stick out your tongue and see if you're telling the truth?"

"Please don't. I really don't know anything. They give me a name. I go get the money."

"So maybe she never stole the money. For all you know, she may never have been in your casino."

"No. She took the money. Look, I know how self-serving this sounds, but you really need to let me go."

"You'll let the five million dollars slide, won't come back again."

"I might."

"I think the knife would stick to your tongue on that one."

"I know I'm in a weak position here, but the logic is irrefutable. You need to give me the money, untie me, and let me go."

"Sounds better for you than for me. Plus I don't have the money."

"What are you going to do? Kill me?" he said. "People know I was here. Kill me, and it's just a question of whether my people or the police get to you first. Which brings us to your second bad option: the police. You can't call the police; explain to them that I'm here because your wife robbed a casino and did God-knows-what-else."

"True," I said.

"Your only choice is to let me go, and give me the money. Money we both know you have."

I looked at the ghostly face staring in the kitchen window.

"Maybe one more choice."

CHAPTER 22

I let Ahlstrom in the back door.

"Where the heck were you earlier?" I said.

"Outside, watching, where I told you I'd be."

"You were just going to let him kill me?"

Ahlstrom shrugged. "Thought you might confess." He paused. "First."

"Some personal cop."

Ahlstrom came up behind Owl, wound up and kicked him in the butt, not a polite joke but a full launch-your-ass-to-the-moon explosion. Owl bounced across the floor and said nothing. Ahlstrom giggled.

"Let me guess," said Owl. "White Portland PD officer, tough as long as your back is turned and you're tied up. His idea of a fair fight, like when we had bows and arrows and his kind had Sharps rifles."

"Don't fight fair with perps, they deserve what they get," said Ahlstrom.

I pointed at Owl. "Waiting for me when I got home. Threatened to fry my tongue with a hot knife."

"Jesus, Chief." He prodded Owl with his boot. "You know how many charges you got against you already? You going to be in jail until you redskins take the country back."

"Or until you make a legitimate arrest," said Owl.

Ahlstrom laughed. "Long wait, anymore, for that."

He turned to me. "When I got here, he already had you tied

up. He say why he wanted to treat you so mean?"

"Thought I had five million dollars."

"Five million dollars?" He looked at me, then at Owl. Then he started laughing and couldn't stop.

"You poor dumb asshole," he poked Owl in the ass again. "He ain't got the five million."

He bent down and put his mouth to Owl's ear. "I do."

He stood up.

"Least whys, the people I work for have the five million, and ain't going to give it to him."

We all stood there in silence for a minute.

I said, "He's talking about a different five million."

Ahlstrom looked at me. We all stood there in silence for another minute.

"Jesus Christ," said Ahlstrom. "How many five-million-dollar bills you got stashed?"

"I don't have his five million. Or yours. Or anybody's."

"White man lies," said Owl. "He's got the tribe's money."

"Well, he doesn't have my company's money."

"That's the point," I said. I was ready for them both to go away. All of this to go away. "I don't have his money. Don't want your money. You two need to talk. Leave me out of this."

Ahlstrom thought about it. "Yeah. We want to talk. If I untie you, you're not going to try to take a knife to me are you?"

"No," said Owl. "And my word is worth something."

Ahlstrom chuckled. "Sure it is. Perps never lie." He looked at the tape. "Jesus Christ, McClaron, are you part spider or something? Looks like you were wrapping this guy up to eat later. Give me that knife."

I handed Ahlstrom the knife and he started cutting. He steadied his hand on Owl's forearm and left it there contemplating his pale hand on Owl's dark skin for a minute before he went back to cutting.

When Ahlstrom had Owl's hands free, Owl said, "I can do the rest."

"I don't mind," said Ahlstrom.

"Here," said Owl. "Let me turn around and make your job easier." He sat up and looked at Ahlstrom.

"Martin Ahlstrom," he said.

"You know me?" said Ahlstrom.

"Of course. You're famous," said Owl.

Ahlstrom snorted. "I'm a washed-up pain in the ass."

"You were famous, back about ten years ago."

"Oh yeah, got my picture in the paper and everything."

"You got more than that. You opened a closed case on the death of a young girl, found the guy that did it after everybody else had given up. They even made a TV movie about it."

Owl looked at me. "You don't know about him?"

"Don't watch many TV movies. Or the news, for that matter."

He turned back to Ahlstrom, looking like a fan boy asking for an autograph. "What was that line?" he said.

Ahlstrom smiled. "Perps always pay."

"Yeah, that's the line that did it for me, the quote every paper in the country used for you. I followed your career since then. You always get the perp. Every time. That's what got me into this business."

"Breaking into houses, torturing people?"

"No, I'm a debt collector. I was working with a group of casinos, doing mathematical modeling of payouts to catch cheaters. Paid well, but I was bored. I took your article into my boss and told him, 'This is what I want to be. Put me in charge of collecting bad debts and thefts, and I'll get every one.' Told him I'd be the Indian Martin Ahlstrom, always get the perp. And I do. You're the man who inspired me."

Ahlstrom stood there. "Imagine that. I don't believe I've ever inspired anyone before."

"Oh, I'm sure it happens all the time. People are probably too intimidated by you to admit it."

"Yeah, that's it." Ahlstrom smiled the first genuine, relaxed smile I had seen on him. "Never figured that out, till now."

He went back to cutting tape with his free hand resting on Owl's knee.

"There," he said. "You're a free man."

"We all are," said Owl. "In our hearts."

I snorted but Ahlstrom nodded gravely.

"Can we move on from this Hallmark moment?" I said. "Figure this thing out and get you two out of my house?"

"Sure. Think you could make us some coffee?"

They sat down at the table and I got out the coffee beans and went to work.

"So how did you find out about the five million?" Ahlstrom said.

"He stole it from us."

Pause.

"You lost me. How do you steal insurance money that hasn't been paid yet?"

"Don't know about that. He stole five million from the casino. Or his wife did. Who knows, he probably helped. We didn't know who she was until I saw her picture in the Portland paper last week trying to sell some of her paintings. Came here to collect."

I looked at Owl.

"Marta stole five million dollars?"

Ahlstrom laughed. "So this guy's tied up in fraud, maybe murder, and now grand theft. Got to hand it to you, pal."

I sat the coffee down.

"I don't believe it," I said.

"Yeah," said Ahlstrom to Owl. "What proof have you got?"

"All you want, at the casino."

Ahlstrom said, "Sounds like we need a road trip."

"Leave me out," I said.

Owl gave a little shake, no, at Ahlstrom.

"I think you better come with us," said Ahlstrom.

Chapter 23

I spent the night handcuffed to my bed with the two of them downstairs while we all tried to get some sleep before going to the casino in the morning. I told them to search all they wanted, satisfy themselves that there were no five million dollar bills or missing wives anywhere. Just don't tear anything up. But every time I woke up, I heard them chattering like a slumber party except that the stories weren't about cute boys and sororities but about weapons and breaking body parts. In the morning, Ahlstrom was a hyperactive ghost, piling the kitchen table high with supplies for what he called the "road trip."

"Put the beer back," I said.

"Ah, come on."

"I'm driving, so I'm not drinking, and I'm not buying beer for two guys who want to put me in jail or worse."

I called Bob and told him to hold down the store. Started to tell him who I was going with but decided that wasn't necessary.

"OK, children," I said. "Into the car."

"Shotgun," yelled Ahlstrom.

"Unless you want it," he said to Owl. "You can have it if you want it."

"No, that's fine. You take it."

We weren't out of the neighborhood before Ahlstrom said, "Hey, can we go to a drive-through, get some coffee and breakfast?"

"No, we can't, for Pete's sake. You should have eaten at the house. Besides, you've got half of my pantry piled on the seat next to Owl. And we're not stopping for a bathroom break. It's only a two-hour drive."

"I told you." Ahlstrom turned back to Owl. "This guy can be a pain."

"You're calling me a pain?" I said. I glanced over and Ahlstrom was grinning, not a grin to trick you up but just a happy-to-be-alive look. "What got into you?"

He giggled and pointed to the back. "You tell him."

Owl said, "I just told him, 'you are not a perp.' "

"Can you imagine that?" said Ahlstrom. "Smartest thing I ever heard, 'you are not a perp.' All my life, walking around ashamed for everything I ever felt or wanted. Let other people make fun of me, call me a ghost cause I'm so pale, make fun of my name, call me 'ass storm.' Just took it and felt guilty about everything I did, like I was a perp that needed to be caught and punished. A wise man comes along and says, 'you are not a perp' and my whole world opens up. You know that 'Owl' is the symbol of wisdom?"

"Seems more like the symbol for 'thug with a hot knife.' " I pulled out onto the highway. "I'm happy for you, Ahlstrom. Really. Does this mean that you no longer feel a need to put me in jail?"

"Yes," he said. "Those compulsions are gone. Of course, I still want my five hundred thousand dollars. And I want to keep my perfect record. But now I'm doing it for the right reasons."

"Makes me feel so much better."

"See?" Ahlstrom turned back to Owl. "I told you, this is the world's biggest Boy Scout, a nice guy about everything."

"I was being sarcastic."

"And," said Owl. "There's that matter of the five million you owe me."

"Other than that," said Ahlstrom. "We're your best friends."

They laughed. I didn't.

"We haven't established that I owe you anything. Don't believe that Marta has ever been on your reservation."

"She was on it pretty regularly. Once we came up with her name, we found out that she's been in and out a lot over the six months before the theft."

"So you say."

"So I will show you."

"Marta never was that interested in money."

"Then ask her to give it back," said Ahlstrom.

"You of all people know the problem with that."

"I know the problems with your story." He reached back and motioned at a bag of chips. "I'm probably your only friend but you lie to me about everything. See, you didn't tell me that Marta took her suitcases. I looked. No women's bags in the house."

"They're in the attic. I checked after she disappeared."

"OK. Didn't look there. But you did, right? Figured you had to cover your bases."

"No."

He motioned at the chips again.

Owl said, "Crap food is bad for your heart, Martin. Try these." He passed up a bag of carrots. Ahlstrom took the bag and looked back at me. "Still, we know that I'll break your story down and get to the truth."

"He will, too," said Owl. "He's Martin Ahlstrom."

Ahlstrom turned his head away so Owl couldn't see him grin.

"Well, let's just get to the casino," I said.

We came to the reservation entrance, big neon sign pointing the direction to the casino. The road we were on was wide and smooth, well-maintained and full of the promise of the wealth and the good life that lay just ahead. The roads peeling off the casino road into the reservation were dirt-and-gravel trails. I looked down one of these and saw two trailers huddled together, a knot of old folks sitting on broken lawn chairs in front.

"That," said Owl, "is who you stole from."

"Yeah," said Ahlstrom. "That, and the mob bosses who actually own the casino, and the banks, and the officials who skim off the money, and . . ."

"It's true," said Owl. "Not as much money goes to the tribe as I'd like."

"Hard to tell how much goes where, since the casinos refuse to allow themselves to be audited."

"Tribal land, tribal law," said Owl. "Not subject to Oregon laws on our own land."

"And the tribal council is owned by the casino," said Ahlstrom.

"I try to work for the tribe," said Owl. "Not always successful. Not always proud of some of the things I do."

"You're one of the good guys," said Ahlstrom. "Remember: you are not a perp. We are not perps."

I felt like I could see Owl smile behind me.

"Thanks."

We came to the casino.

"Pull up there," said Owl. We pulled under an awning and a young man held out his hand for my keys.

"I'll park it myself," I said.

Owl got out. "Suit yourself. You'll save us the trouble of breaking into your car when we search it, and save yourself the damage."

I started to say something but he said, "Tribal land, tribal law."

I got out and handed the keys to the kid. I stood there and watched him drive it down the hill into a sheet metal shed tucked into the trees. I turned and followed Ahlstrom and Owl inside.

An important-looking man and a woman who could have been a movie star or a high-class hooker were waiting on Owl. Owl said a few words to them, they nodded and floated off in different directions.

"This way," said Owl. We walked that way through a plush lobby with glittering lights. People in casino uniforms either smiled curtly or got out of the way as Owl came their way. A uniformed man appeared from nowhere and opened an unmarked door. Owl walked through without breaking stride or acknowledging the man.

The room looked like a VIP suite with a flat screen that took up one wall. Owl motioned us to leather theater seats.

The movie star/hooker/hostess came in with a tray of drinks and food. Distributed the food, drinks and a few come-hither smiles and left without a word. Owl motioned behind me. I turned and saw a large scowling young man sitting at my elbow.

"He'll be your escort while we're here," said Owl. "You need anything, just ask him."

"What do I call him?"

"I'd suggest 'sir.' "

Ahlstrom laughed.

Owl nodded and the screen came to life showing a bare steel room with two guys holding automatic weapons flanking a safe.

"Note the date," he said. "The night before your wife's disappearance."

"Or murder," said Ahlstrom. "Some coincidence."

A black-haired woman in a uniform walked into the frame and nodded. One of the men opened the safe while the other watched the woman. Handed her two cloth bags tied together. The woman hoisted the bags over her shoulder, turned and looked full into the camera.

Marta. No disguise, no makeup even. No attempt to avoid the camera or hide. She knew the picture would come out. She knew she would be gone.

"You're saying you just let people walk out with a bag holding five million dollars?" I said.

"We did that day. A trusted courier that the guards are supposed to know personally is supposed to walk in, take one million in hundred-dollar bills from here and walk it down to another room owned by the bank.

"Someone called the guards and told them there was a substitute that day. Your wife made that trip five times. The next day, the bank told us the money they had received was counterfeit. Hand-printed on the wrong kind of paper, but still pretty good. We don't know how she made the switch."

The screen jumped ahead to Marta walking in again. When she turned to the camera this time, Owl nodded and her image froze on the screen.

"But we are sure it was your wife."

So was I. The night of the robbery, Marta had disappeared into her studio and refused to come out. She was gone forever when I woke up the next morning.

I stepped up close to the big screen, Marta's face dominating my vision. I studied her for any clue. I recognized the pose. Marta and Larry fought about it constantly; Larry called it her "driver's license pose" and wouldn't let that pose go out on any of her publicity. Her face was dead and cold, mouth a thin, tight, determined line, eyes blank.

I heard Ahlstrom behind me.

"So your guards just picked up the phone, heard a voice say, 'we're sending somebody you don't know in. She's probably a thief, but give her as many bags of money as she wants. Validate her parking, too.' "

"Pretty much," said Owl.

131

"I take it you weren't in charge of that part of security."

"No. I come in after. The two guards were questioned extensively."

Ahlstrom laughed. "Tribal law?"

"Tribal law."

"Where are they now?"

"No one knows. No one is going to know."

Ahlstrom laughed again. "I like the way your courts work here."

I pointed at the screen. "Go forward. Slow."

Owl nodded and we watched Marta come and go. On the last trip, Marta blew a kiss to the camera.

"Freeze that," I said.

Standing in front of a six-foot tall face of Marta, I could see her eyes were brimming with tears. A kiss and tears, my farewell image of Marta.

CHAPTER 24

"I've seen what I needed," I said. "Let's go home."

"Hey," said Ahlstrom. "So now you admit to one crime?" He nodded deferentially to Owl. "Maybe two, if you count Oregon law and tribal law."

"I admit that's Marta. That's all. I'm done with you guys." My eyes were blurring. I needed to get out of there and I didn't need to share a two hour ride back with them. "Find your own way back." I grabbed the doorknob but it didn't turn. My scowling escort was standing at my elbow.

"I'm afraid your truck isn't ready yet," said Owl.

"What the heck is that supposed to mean? I saw them park it in the shed down the hill."

"Still, we need a few more minutes with it. And we'd like to talk to you for a few minutes, if you don't mind, now that you've seen the videotape with your own eyes."

"Some other time, guys. I'm going back to Portland. Unlock the door. Have Chief Hulking Bull here show me to my car."

"I'm sorry." Owl tried the smile on me. "That won't be possible just yet. But if you'll try that door over there, you'll find it unlocked. We just need a few minutes of your time to answer a few questions, then you can be on your way."

"What is that, the room of the hot knives? Are you going to send me on my way to join the guards?"

"Please don't insult me with your crude stereotypes. We have progressed a little bit. It's just a polygraph machine. We'd like to see how it responds to your answers. Really, it's painless and will only take a few minutes."

Ahlstrom said, "Those things don't always work."

"We also have sodium pentothal."

"I've never seen that stuff used."

Owl lit up. "It's so much fun. The problem is getting the perps to shut up. Really, you're going to be listening to Paul here tell you all about his sixth birthday and how his heart was broken when he didn't get a pony."

He smiled back at me. "If you make us use that, of course. Shall we?"

He gestured to the door and Hulking Bull jerked his chin at the door and I marched, getting a step ahead of them all. I threw open the door and stepped through.

The room could have been a clinic: cool, antiseptic, mint-green walls and stainless steel equipment. An examining table, with straps, was on the wall to my left. In the middle of the room there was something that looked like an electric chair with wires running from it to a cart with electronics. A man in a white lab suit and big reflective glasses sat at the cart, staring at the display in front of him and ignoring us. The only other door was behind him and I guessed it was locked.

To my left, a glass wall looked out over the beach. I guessed we were on the second floor, third tops. If I could land on the soft sand, roll as I hit, I might have a chance.

Hulking Bull pushed me toward the electric chair. I took a step, pivoted, and ran to the window, jumped and spun to put my back to the window and put my hands over my face as I crashed into the window.

When I opened my eyes, I was lying on the floor with their three faces staring down at me. My back and my head hurt.

"That looked like fun," said Ahlstrom.

"It's been a long time since that trick actually worked," said

Owl. "In the old Western movies, they used glass made out of sugar, breaks easily and doesn't cut anyone. The glass they use in modern buildings is stronger than you."

He smiled again. "But I guess you know that now."

Ahlstrom laughed his little "heh-heh-heh" laugh.

Owl bent down and ran his hands over my back and head. I started to slap his hands away but decided playing helpless might help somehow.

"Nothing broken," he said. "Yet. Why don't you sit down and make yourself comfortable?" Hulking Bull picked me up and set me in the electric chair. The man with the big glasses hooked up the wires and cuffs and went back to his seat.

"Huh," he said. "Blood pressure's high."

"We'll be sure to notify his physician," said Owl. Ahlstrom went, "heh-heh-heh."

They asked me my name and address; questions they already knew the answers to. The technician nodded to Owl.

Ahlstrom said, "Let me have the first question."

Owl smiled. "But of course."

Ahlstrom walked around and put his face in mine.

"Is Marta Strauss-McClaron still alive?"

The room grew silent and I looked around in a panic.

I jumped up, wires ripping out of the chair. Hulking Bull grabbed for me. I ducked under him and looked for a way out. I jumped at the technician and he threw his hands up to his face. Hulking Bull was coming back and I looked back and forth between him and the locked door, panicked.

I jumped behind the technician's table and grabbed the sharpest thing I could find: a metal pen. I stood there for a minute, feeling silly, Ahlstrom and Owl starting to laugh at me. I jumped and came up behind Owl, grabbed his arm and jabbed the pen into his neck and held it there. The room froze.

"Maybe this only works in the movies, too," I said. "But I'm pretty sure that if I push a little harder, your carotid artery will shred and you'll bleed to death before help can get here."

Owl didn't flinch. "I'm pretty sure you're right. So what do we do now?"

"First," I said, "we get a door open. Where does that one lead?"

"Hallway."

"Open it."

He nodded and Hulking Bull unlocked the door.

"Now, the rest of you go stand against the window."

I eased Owl back with me and cracked the door open and looked out into an empty hall with nothing in sight either way.

"You have to know," said Owl, "there are cameras everywhere. You won't get far. Look, I'll even help you. Go right, fewer cameras that way, closer to an exit. Assuming you believe me."

I shoved Owl into the room and took off left. Looked up at the video camera at the end of the hall and took the next left. Two men in suits got off an elevator, pointed, and started running toward me. I ran the other way and heard shouts.

I saw a service cart in the hall with a white tablecloth draped to the floor. I ducked under the cart and the tablecloth and hid. A man ran by and didn't stop.

I stayed there until my breathing settled down. I was about to peek out from the sheet when the cart started moving. Holding on, I duck-walked backwards and tried to stay with the cart. When we got to the elevator, I tripped on the elevator threshold and almost went down. Whoever was pushing the cart thought it was stuck and shoved it hard into the elevator and trapped me between the cart and the wall and I moaned.

The cart-pusher didn't care. The elevator moved down, stopped, and then the cart started to move back. I scrunched down, let the cart and its tablecloth pull away from me and hoped the cart-pusher was watching the hall.

He was. I punched every floor button I could see and didn't breathe until the doors closed. When the doors opened, I peeked out. No one in sight. I jumped out and tried the first door I saw.

Stepped into a long room with mirrors and makeup stands on the left and rows of costumes on the right. Showgirls' dressing room, empty. I thought I heard voices in the hall and ducked back into the dresses and held my breath until I was sure I was alone.

Chapter 25

I looked at the withered old farmer feeding the quarter slots and he stared back like he had never seen anything like the vision floating his way. I was football-player tall, dressed in a full dress of rhinestones, with pale pancake makeup and long, flowing flame-red hair. I tottered toward him on high platform sandals, my head held high and haughty, ignoring the pain of the mincing little steps.

He threw back the rest of his Wild Turkey.

"How much, honey?"

He tugged at the dress. He could only reach my ass, but it was high enough.

"How much, honey?"

In my best falsetto, I said, "You can't afford me."

"I got money, honey. I know I don't look like much . . ."

I walked away, almost toppling over with every step. He caught me at the door and pulled on my dress again.

"Honey, please."

"Oh, for goodness sakes," I said in my real voice. "What in tarnation is wrong with you?"

He still followed me out the door, past two security guards scanning the door. I stopped in the parking lot and pulled off the ridiculous platform sandals and threw them at the farmer.

"Leave me alone," I screamed in a falsetto.

He picked up the shoes like they were treasure.

I glanced at the guards. They were paying no attention. This was normal for them in this world, I guessed. They were watching for something crazy, like a guy in khakis and a blue work shirt.

I walked barefoot down the service road past the shed where they had taken my truck. Ducked into the woods and came up around the back.

There was a big open door in the back with The Beast sitting just inside. The men inside seemed to have gotten word that I was coming and were gathered at the front window watching the casino doors.

I crept up and looked in the truck. The keys were in the ignition. I eased the door open, got in and cranked the engine while I was still ducked down out of sight.

The men came running, one of them pounding on my window. I put The Beast in drive and popped up in his face and he jumped back. The last thing he saw as the truck roared away was a big redhead with too much makeup and a terrified look on her face.

I wasn't alone long. The rear view mirror filled up with two casino pickup trucks behind me and uniformed men pouring out of the casino like angry ants from an anthill. I turned hard at the first left and lost the two trucks. I stopped at an overlook where I could see the turnoff but they couldn't see me. The next car stayed on the main road, but the sedan following him turned down my road. In the distance, I could see the trucks turning around and coming back to follow the sedan. And me.

"Dang it," I said. Floored my truck back out onto the road and took every random turn I could. Every time I could look back, the sedan was still there with the other cars and trucks behind him.

I took a dirt trail, then swung off on a smaller cattle road with a barbed-wire fence and a metal gate standing open. I backed my truck into a little stand of brush and got out. If they could follow me in here, I was going to have to go on foot and hope I could outrun them, which might be tricky in bare feet. I snuck through the brush and up a little hill where I could hide and watch.

I pulled the dress over my head and saw a man standing by a tree watching me.

"You people are crazy here," was all he said.

I stood there with a glittering dress in my hands and a red wig at my feet and wondered where to start. He reached into a back pocket and pulled out a neatly-folded handkerchief.

"You may want this."

He was very tall and very thin and very black. His accent was French. He pointed to the makeup on my face. I wiped it off and offered the handkerchief back. He laughed.

"Why don't you keep it? I really don't want to explain to my wife why I have makeup on my wipe. Not sure that telling her it came from a barefoot man dressed as a woman would help much."

I looked down the hill and saw cars and trucks pulling up next to mine, men getting out.

"Friends of yours?" he said.

"No."

"I didn't think so."

I looked at his arm. It had three slashes.

"Leongo?"

"Yes."

I said, "I knew a man from Leongo who had the same tattoo."

"You did not know him well, or you would not call this a tattoo. Child soldiers came to our neighborhood, forcing the male children to join them. The leaders in this army mark people for death with three slashes of the machete on the forearm. The new recruit is supposed to prove himself by finishing the job by cutting off the head of the man with the slashes. So, if your friend has this mark, he was marked for death, and he would not call this a tattoo."

"How did you survive?"

"The new child soldier refused to kill me and my wife, so they killed him." He paused a long time.

"He was our oldest son. Because he refused to kill us, they killed him and let us live. Ironic, don't you think, that our son died to save us?"

"Heroic," I said. "Tragic. But I don't see . . ."

"Here is the irony: the army that killed my son call themselves 'Warriors for Christ' and the leader is the 'Man from God.' They receive support from some cowards in America because they kill Moslems and therefore must be good Christians. Now, I have become a believer in the true Christ myself, and when I see the body on the cross, I think of my son."

He looked at me. "And I try to repay."

He pulled a cell phone from his pocket and called someone. When he put the phone back in his pocket, he pointed at a neighboring hill.

"My younger son is gathering our cattle on that hill. Watch."

A young boy ran out of a thicket on the top of the hill, screaming and pointing back. Most of the men at the cars rushed to follow his agitated pointing. Only one man stayed with the cars.

"Come," my new friend said. "We must move quickly."

We crept down the hill to the cars. I picked up a heavy stick, snuck up behind the guard, and hit him on the head.

"I'm sorry," I said to him lying on the ground. "I had to."

The Leongolian laughed and bent over the man.

"You are not much of a desperado, I'm afraid." He felt the man's head. "He will be all right soon. You do not hit so very hard."

He looked up at me. "I was a veterinarian, back home. The group that paid for me asked me how I wanted to live, and I chose to be a cattle rancher here."

He saw I needed more.

"There is a group that buys hostages from the Warriors and finds them homes. Some say they are helping the Warriors by giving them money for ammunition. People like me say they are the angels of God."

We stood there a minute.

"You must go," he said. "I will close the gate behind you. It will delay them, but not for long."

I got in the truck and leaned out the window.

"Do you know," I said, "a woman named Marta . . . black hair, very intense?"

His eyes grew wide.

"God be with you."

I left and took back roads toward Portland, stopping once to find some spare boots in the back of the truck. Halfway there, I stopped in a motel in a small town rather than go home. I didn't sleep much. Every time I looked out the window, I thought I saw a car go by slowly, watching.

CHAPTER 26

I drove straight into Larry's office Thursday morning without going to the house or the shop. Gwen smiled at me as I walked in and waved me straight into his office.

"Thanks for getting here so fast," Larry said.

I looked at him and started to ask him what he meant. Gwen yelled from behind my back. "I haven't talked to him yet, Larry. Left a dozen messages everywhere, but haven't talked to him."

I pulled my cell out of my pocket. It was dead.

"Oh," I said.

"You need to pay attention," Larry said. "I'm not going to have another Marta, never around when I need her."

"You have my sympathy," I said. "Can't imagine what that's like."

He stopped with his mouth open, about to say something.

"Sorry," he said.

"It's OK. Got bigger problems than being offended now."

"Damned right," he said. He stopped again and looked at me.

"No, wait, why did you come in here, if you didn't come because Gwen called?"

"I need to report a kidnapping. A kidnapping that we don't need to report."

Larry put his hands in his church-steeple-listening pose.

"You obviously aren't the victim. Marta?"

"No. What's wrong with you? It can't be Marta. You're the

one who keeps telling me I need to accept she's gone. Now you think she's kidnapped?"

He stayed in his pose and said nothing.

"Well it was me," I said. "You ever think I could be the one that crazy things happen to?"

"A kidnap victim," he said. "And yet, here you sit."

"I got away."

He laughed. "Sorry. You're not exactly James Bond."

"I got away. Dressed in drag."

"Please don't put that image in my mind."

"Helped by an African refugee on an Indian reservation."

"Did you, by any chance, have mushrooms with your dinner last night?"

I gave him a look and he threw up his hands.

"Hey, this is Portland. Everyone does pharmaceuticals here. The Welcome Wagon puts dime bags of grass in the welcome baskets."

"Not me. You know I've got a two-beer limit."

"Doesn't sound like it right now."

"Just listen."

I told him the story and he listened, nodding occasionally. At the end, he said, "Gwen?"

"Already checked," came her voice. "Nobody named 'Owl' works for Four Winds. No record of any Leongolian cattle farmers on the reservation, but who knows."

"Well, that's one thing we can take care of," said Larry. "I'll talk to the chief of police when we get done here. Ahlstrom's ass is fired."

"Too late. He's retired, gone to work for the insurance company chasing one case."

"He's off the books," called Gwen, "but they've opened an expense account in his name."

"Christ," said Larry. He said some other words, too, not

nearly as nice. "If you drove them, it's not kidnapping. And this guy Owl is right; Indian law is sovereign on the reservation."

"So what does this not–James Bond do?"

Larry's steeple-fingers were down now and drumming on his desk.

"Dunno. You're no James Bond, but I'm not 'M' either. Just a humble purveyor of fine art, with no answers here. Reminds me." He pulled out a printed sheet. "This is why I called you."

I took the sheet and looked at it. There were eight small pictures of paintings. Marta paintings.

"I've never seen these." I put the sheet on his desk.

"Neither have I. Gallery owner in Meteor, Arizona claims they're real, plans to put them up for sale next month."

The pictures lay on the desk between us.

"Are they real?" I said.

Larry shrugged.

"How old are they supposed to be?"

"Red Rock—that's the name of the gallery—owner says they are recent. Won't say how he came across them."

"So what do we do?"

"Owner wants me to come to Meteor, authenticate that the paintings are Marta's. I don't have time. I'm going to send Don Johns, the art appraiser I work with."

"Don doesn't know Marta's work. Don doesn't know Marta."

"No."

We both sat there and stared at the pictures and thought our thoughts.

"I'll go," I said. "I need to get out of town for a while anyway, since my lawyer can't protect me from being not-kidnapped."

Larry didn't say anything. I picked up the pictures. I had once said that I would not search for Marta, would live without knowing the answers.

Now I said, "I'll see what I can find."

CHAPTER 27

I was tired of other people and other things defining my life.

"Starting over," I told Bob. We were standing in front of a rack of river pants, quick drying nylon khakis that had legs that could be zipped off to make them shorts if I wanted. I took the tags off of three of them and dropped the tags into a plastic bag Bob was holding. I rolled the pants up and put them in the duffel bag I had already taken off the shelf.

"Not even going home," I said. I didn't mention that there might be Indians and ghost-pale unemployed detectives waiting for me there. Sounded crazy even to me.

"I don't know, Paul. Seems pretty severe to me. I mean, you've got a pretty good life here. Nice house and everything. I think I'd go home, pack my own clothes, take a few days off . . ."

"New clothes," I said. I picked a blue fishing shirt off a rack.

"My computer . . ."

"I'll buy a new one on the way out of town. Everything new."

"New car?"

I looked out the window at The Beast.

"No. Keeping The Beast."

"Might want to swing by the house, pick up a memento to remind you of what you and Marta meant to each other."

I thought about that long enough that Bob started to shuffle.

"Yeah. Want to find something to tell me what Marta and I mean to each other."

Either Bob didn't catch the change of tense or he was deep in don't-upset-the-crazy-person mode.

"I can look after the store until you get back," he said. "I've got your cell."

"And the address of the timeshare I've rented in Meteor. Won't be there for a week or so, though. Going to explore the country on the way down."

"Good for you, Paul. I really think a vacation will do you good. Just don't do anything wild and crazy."

I just smiled.

We strapped the new kayak on the roof of The Beast and walked back inside. I pointed to the pile of tags on the counter.

"Add it up, put that on my account, please."

"Sure." He shuffled awkwardly.

I put out my hand.

"Might be a few weeks or more before I return. Maybe longer. I'll stay in touch but I couldn't do this without knowing I could count on you here. Thanks."

He shook my hand and shuffled some more. "Take care of yourself."

I laughed.

Bob held my hand a little too long and said, "I hope that's an easy job now."

I stopped at the big shopping center on the way out of town. Bought underwear, toothbrush, went to the electronics store and bought a shiny metal laptop from a bouncy teen-aged clerk with bright eyes who was proud to tell me that my new machine could play Masters of Doom with a benchmark of some obviously-impressive number. I didn't care, but I didn't argue.

"Cool," I said. "Can I do email and get The Weather Channel on it?"

His face fell, "Well, you can do that on anything. But this is a really good machine, sir."

"Good. I'll take it."

I stopped at a local coffee shop for my last cup of Portland coffee for a while. When I crossed into the eastern slope of the Cascades, heading downhill with the whole world spread out before me, I glanced at the seat and saw a brand-new guide book to rivers of the western US, an empty cup, and nothing else. I smiled and felt at home, and looked into the distance.

The next morning, first light, I was at the put-in for the river I had wanted to explore before my life got busy. I couldn't take a week to explore it, but I was going to take a day. There was a part-time hipster kid with narrow curly sideburns that met in a point on his chin, hanging around on the weekend to see if anybody needed a guide.

"Don't need a guide," I said. "But I might have a way you can make money."

"I'm all ears, pops."

"From here," I pointed at the river map under the glass counter, "if I leave now, where is a good place to come out in the afternoon? Late afternoon."

"Depends, man. Newbie, maybe here." He put a finger down on the map.

"I'm new to this river, but I know kayaks and rivers."

He studied me and made up his mind.

"Here." His finger moved down the map. "Most beautiful part of the whole river. Great place to come out."

"I'll give you a hundred dollars to take my truck down there and wait for me."

He looked at me with contempt. "No, man, way too much. I can get Zach to follow me down and bring me back. Stick you for twenty."

"No. My truck has my whole life in it. Want you to stay in sight of it until I get there."

He thought about it and brightened. "Yeah, man. There's a

cool little eating spot there, with Wi-Fi. I can hang out, catch up on my school work. Good deal."

It was a dazzling river, or maybe just a dazzling day. Too soon, I came to the restaurant with The Beast in the parking lot. I pulled out and walked up. The hipster was packing his laptop into a backpack.

"Hey," he said as I paid him. "Two friends of yours came by, said to tell you hi."

I froze, hand in mid-air with his last twenty. He must have taken it as hesitation to pay.

"Hey, I did what you told me, cat. Looked out and saw them eyeballing your ride, marched out and told them to stay away or I'd whomp them. They just smiled, said they were friends. Got in their car and drove away."

I handed him the twenty.

"What did they look like?"

"White, white guy and an old Indian chief."

CHAPTER 28

I got the description of Ahlstrom and Owl's car from the hipster and went on down the road. Intentionally took a couple of wrong turns, then headed up a winding mountain road and stopped at an overlook and sat on the hood of The Beast sipping on a water bottle and watching the road below.

It only took ten minutes. I saw the black Mercedes start up the mountain, slow and pull into an overlook below me. I waited another twenty minutes but no one got out of the Mercedes to enjoy the scenery. When I passed the overlook on the way down the mountain, the Mercedes was gone. Somehow, the Mercedes had known to stop when I stopped, and leave when I started moving.

I checked into a small rural motel and thought about what to do next. The next day I drove until I found what I was looking for on the outskirts of Vegas: two motels across the street from each other, one with a Waffle House next door. I pulled into the one across the street from the Waffle House and parked. In half an hour I saw the Mercedes pull into the other motel and check in. I checked into my motel and got a good night's sleep.

The next morning, I sat watching out the motel window until I saw Ahlstrom and Owl walk across to the Waffle House. Put my bag in The Beast and joined them.

Ahlstrom and Owl sat together on one side of the booth giggling at each other. I slid into the other side.

"Just coffee," I said to the waitress. I smiled.

Owl was impassive. Ahlstrom smiled back. "See, I told you this guy is smart. He knows we're on his side."

"Except when you want to put me in jail," I said. "Or when he wants to kill me to get his money."

"Just business," said Owl. "If we don't get our money soon, this will get ugly."

"Hey, I don't even have enough money for breakfast," I said.

"I do," grinned Ahlstrom. "The insurance company pays expenses."

"So you've got a paid vacation until we resolve this," I said. "You're in no hurry."

"Yeah," he said, looking at Owl. "This is the best time of my life."

"Speaking of life," I said. "You guys may want to take care of mine. I'm your best lead. Anything happens to me, you both lose."

I looked out the window at an eighteen wheeler getting ready to pull out from my motel. I stood up.

"Time to go," I said.

Ahlstrom paid and we walked out into the parking lot.

"So we'll just stay behind you today," said Ahlstrom. "Not bother with staying out of sight. Maybe meet up for lunch."

"Sure," I said, watching the eighteen wheeler pull away. Mentally said goodbye to the GPS transmitter I had taken off The Beast and put on the eighteen wheeler.

"You might," I said to Owl, "want to fix that flat tire on the Mercedes before you leave."

Heard them cursing as I pulled away. I stayed behind the eighteen wheeler until he pulled up onto the interstate, then I skirted the north side of Vegas and headed across the desert.

Some people in Portland don't like the desert; talk about all the things that aren't there. Today, it seemed like an empty palette full of possibilities. As I drove, I imagined what it would look like with cactus blooming and wildflowers on fire with color under endless blue skies. Passed through the mountain forests around Flagstaff, the pines standing straight and silent like the sentinels of God. Just outside of Sedona, the nearest big town to Meteor, I stopped in an overlook on a creek and watched kids in tubes splashing through clear cold water.

I drove into Sedona and took the road up a hill to the airport. There's a ritual in Sedona of locals and tourists gathering at a place near the airport to watch the sunset. The place is said to be blessed with a special energy. Standing there that night, watching the sun's colors flow over Sedona's red rock hills shaped like a coffee pot and a sugar loaf, I felt like the air was full of possibilities waiting for me.

I drove down the hill and out of Sedona to the condo in Meteor as the light was fading. I walked smiling up to the registration desk and gave the man my name.

"Oh, your wife has already checked in," he said.

CHAPTER 29

The incense should have tipped me off. I stood in the open condo door in the fading evening light, desert air cooling around me, key in hand, afraid to walk through this door, and smelled sandalwood. It registered as being out of place, but my mind was racing in too many directions to pay it any mind.

"Ommmm."

I opened the door and heard the sound more as a high, clear vibration than a word.

"Ommmm."

Rue was sitting in the middle of the darkened living room floor, chanting cross-legged as a wisp of incense drifted up past her head. She was naked.

"Ommmm." She opened her eyes. Smiled a Cheshire-cat smile at me, rose in one smooth motion, floated over to the couch and slid a silky one-piece dress/robe thing over her head and let it fall down and mostly cover her body, at least to the top of her legs.

"I thought you'd never get here," she said.

I ran through a list of answers and didn't find any good ones.

She giggled. "I've never seen a man look so disappointed to find a naked woman waiting for him."

"No, it's not . . . I mean, you're very . . ." I paused. "I don't mean to sound rude, but what are you doing here?"

She sat down on the couch, crossed her legs and sipped from a water bottle.

"I heard you talking to Bob. I thought about everything I've heard about this area being a center for enlightenment, and thought it would be a good place for me to come start my own kayak shop."

"We're in a desert."

"A desert with Oak Creek running through it, and the Verde River a few miles away. I thought you might help me get started. It seemed like a perfect opportunity."

"You don't have a car. How'd you get here ahead of me?"

"I took the universal transit system." She put out her thumb. "Direct connection via a trucker to Phoenix, then north to Meteor with a spiritual counselor and a songwriter who writes songs with just one note. Great for meditation."

"Sounds like wild party music."

"You're probably wondering why I'm here, in our condo."

"I was kind of wondering how it got to be 'our' condo."

"I got here a lot faster than you did." She paused. "Really, you should sell The Beast and just hitch. It's much more efficient."

"Easy to take a kayak, too."

She waved that away. "People make room for stuff. You'd be surprised."

"I'm surprised at a lot of things lately."

"So when I got here, I called around to see where you'd be staying."

"I'm surprised you have a phone rather than relying on psychic friends."

"Of course I use a phone. You've got to have a smartphone. How else are you going to surf the web when you're hitching?"

"How indeed."

"So the office here said you had a unit rented but hadn't checked in."

"I rented it early. Didn't know when I'd get in."

"See? Private transit is just so unreliable and outdated."

"I'm old-fashioned like that."

"You are. So I asked the woman and she said the unit had two bedrooms. I would have been happy with one, but I know you're still working through some things about us. I thought that was a clear message from the universe if I've ever heard one."

"Of course."

"So I hiked over, told them I was your wife, and checked in."

"They didn't ask for any proof?"

"This is Meteor," she said. "More open-minded even than Portland. What do you think, they're going to demand a marriage license before they let two people share a place?"

I started to say what I thought, but she went on.

"I think it is so sweet how 1950s you are."

"I'm not that old."

"I meant your soul. People say I have an old soul, too. Spiritually, I'm probably older than you."

"I'm probably your spiritual grandson," I said.

Rue frowned. "No, we're not related. That would get icky."

"Icky or not, that's how I'm going to think of you if you're going to stay here." I pointed at the kitchen. "Is there beer at Grandma's house?"

"Yes. No. Yes, there is beer. No, don't call me 'Grandma.' "

I went in and got a Tecate. Good choice. I walked back in and sat down in the chair opposite Rue.

"Do you prefer 'Nana'?"

"No. Things are complicated enough between us. Let's not throw that in."

"Maybe 'Me-Maw'?"

"No. Look, I'll make you a deal. You're not comfortable with me naked. I'm not comfortable with being called 'Grandma.' You don't call me 'Grandma,' and I won't walk around naked."

She hesitated. "Much."

I smiled. "No deal." I was surprised at how comfortable I was with this. And with Rue. "Walk around naked all you want. You make naked look good, both in the wink-wink-boy-is-she-hot kind of way, and the way some women make a dress look beautiful. I'm not going to lie to you or myself about my enjoying you naked. I just can't do anything about it now."

"That's a major admission from you. You're getting in touch with your feelings." She was trying to play therapist, but I could see her smile.

"Personal growth is painful," I said. "Some people torture themselves to work through their problems. I learn to tolerate naked women." I felt myself smiling. "A naked woman," I corrected. "You."

We both smiled bigger but then it felt awkward.

"So," she said, getting serious and changing the subject. "Are you ready to talk about those things you can't talk about?"

I thought. "More like those things I don't know about. Perhaps it's time to talk about some of those."

Rue smiled at the invitation and nodded wisely. "It's hard to know with certainty about what comes . . . after. No matter what we believe, we struggle with certainty."

"No, I don't mean death . . . well, it is about certainty of a kind, I guess."

She nodded. "Closure. About what you believe happens when a loved one moves on. Can we talk about your religious tradition?"

I laughed, even though it wasn't funny. It just seemed that some people looked at my life these days and saw fraud, and Rue saw God. I wasn't sure who was right.

"I don't know," I said. "I respect everybody's beliefs." I paused. "But that doesn't make them mine." I sat there thinking, and Rue gave me time.

"I guess I believe you deserve what you build with your own two hands."

"Karma," she said.

"Or carpentry," I said.

I stood up.

"C'mon," I said. "We can talk later. Right now, we have something we need to do."

CHAPTER 30

"Walking therapy," said Rue. "I like it. Maybe I could write a book, *Walking, Talking Therapy.*"

We were walking west toward the last light of sunset. There was still enough light to see the darkening red of Coffee Pot Rock and Sugar Loaf Rock in the distance in Sedona. That was what they called the rock formations here, just "rocks." I liked the cleanness of that. Bigger than hills, smaller than mountains, this area was a desert littered with strange red rock formations that weren't quiet mesas or anything else. John Wayne western movie country. So we walked toward a red rock coffee pot taller than most skyscrapers, and a sugar loaf standing next to it. They felt like details left behind by a giant, playful artist and I felt comforted walking in their shadow with Rue.

"OK," she said. "So now you do the 'talking' part."

She had looped one arm through mine and we were bumping against each other as we walked.

"Maybe later. Maybe over dinner. First, I need to go to a gallery up here. The owner says he has some new paintings of Marta's."

She stopped. Her hand was like a vice on my arm so I stopped, too.

"New paintings?" she said. "I thought—"

"A lot of people thought that. I don't know what to think. That's why I'm here." I paused. "Probably why other people will be here soon, too."

She picked up her walk and dragged me along.

"We do need to talk," she said.

"We do. Over dinner. First, I need to see these paintings."

"Yeah. Be interesting to see how new these are."

"And if they're Marta's," I said.

"Yeah."

I saw a Bashas' grocery store and turned in at the strip mall beside it, found a tiny storefront with "Jingle Records" in funky hand-painted letters. Next to it was a bigger store with the windows covered with displays showing prints of Meteor scenery, cowboy statues and Native American artifacts. The sign said, "Red Rock Gallery."

A bell tinkled over the door as we pushed in and stood in an entry room with the walls covered with paintings. I was saying something to Rue as we stepped in the door but I was immediately struck silent, forgot what it was we'd been discussing.

I stood there holding my breath, mentally wrapped up in the old familiar colors of the brand new paintings. Rue slipped her arm out of mine and pulled out her smartphone. "I'll take some pictures."

I felt years and memories and smells and certainties come back again as if they had never left, the last six months gone as if they had never happened.

"These are real," I said. Or maybe whispered, half-lost in my own head.

Someone rustled in the next room. I was sure it was Marta, and I felt guilty about the ways I had wanted to move on without her. Needed to apologize.

A foot stepped into the room and I was already saying, "I'm sorry," and my eyes were blurring. They focused on a balding, crooked little man who looked like a minor villain in an old western, right down to a leather vest.

"Closing early, folks," he said. Dismissed us with a frowning wave and turned away. "Sorry."

Rue stepped in front of him.

"Do you know who this is?"

"Don't give a damn if he's a rat turd or the pope. Get out."

"This is Paul McClaron."

"Good for him."

She waved around the room. "Marta Strauss-McClaron?"

"Oh." He straightened up as much as he could and plastered a big you-got-something-I-want smile on.

"I'm Roger Crosswinds. I am surely glad to see you, Mr. Mc-Claron." He grabbed my hand hanging limp at my side and jerked it up and down like it was a pump in the desert and he was a thirsty man. He finally let go and dropped it back in place.

"What do you think?" He waved at the walls.

I studied the eager crooked man.

"I think I need some time to analyze these."

"Of course, of course. But your first impression is that they're the real deal?"

I stared down at him for a long time. "I don't make first impressions."

"Of course, of course. I'm sorry, sir, but I really am closing right now. Family emergency, and I've got to get out of here in a hurry. Could you come back tomorrow morning, say nine o'clock?"

I looked at the swirling colors on the walls.

"Of course."

CHAPTER 31

Rue and I stood on the sidewalk as the gallery door clicked shut behind us.

"What's next?" she said. "Tonight, I mean."

"Dinner, I guess." My mind's eye was still focused on the paintings locked behind us.

"Where?"

"Don't care. You pick."

She put her hands on her hips. "Get your draggy ass off the ground and make a decision."

"Oh, I don't know. Somewhere comfortable. Meat, potatoes. Anywhere's fine."

"Listen to your therapist. Pick."

"Not sure I signed up for this therapy."

"Sure you did. You fall in the water, you need to be saved. Now, look in your heart. Find something you want to do, but that your habits tell you not to do."

"OK." I smiled for no reason. "I'm going weird. Remember the diner we passed right after we left the condo? One with the big radio beacon and statues of aliens waving hello in the front yard?"

Rue squealed, "Yes. The Beacon. There was a UFO sighting here a couple of years ago; the owners remodeled their diner to welcome the visitors they were sure were going to come. The Beacon broadcasts a welcoming greeting they say will call the UFO back. That's where I've wanted to go ever since I saw it."

She grabbed my arm and dragged me down the street.

"Six months," she said. "Give me six months, and we'll get you free of your demons. You know, we're starting to develop a connection."

"Maybe a little," I said. I thought of the paintings and pulled her arm away.

She was almost skipping. My long legs ate up two of her strides with each one of my own but it was still hard to keep up with her.

"You know flying saucers are real," she said. "In 1948, they landed a couple of hundred miles from here and the establishment killed the occupants rather than listen to their message of peace and enlightenment."

"And there goes the connection. You're sure I'm the one who needs therapy?"

The Beacon had statues of an alien family out front with hands up waving at the tourists on Main Street. Impossibly tall, impossibly thin, odd-skinned and sad-eyed, they looked as out of place—alienated, I guess—as I felt as they waved at cars that never waved back. We walked in, past a poster of an alien with a caption of "I'm only here for the beer." A hulking Goth boy with a name tag that said "Rick" handed us two menus and said in a flat voice, "Welcome to the universe."

Rue's jaw dropped and she turned on me.

"See? I knew it. There is a headquarters, and we've found it. This is where the voices in my head come from. Must be broadcasting from the tower."

Rick just stood there with his pencil on his pad and no expression on his face. I ordered a Carne Asada Burrito and Rue ordered a Falafel Sandwich. Rick sighed like we had ordered the worst things on the menu and dragged himself away.

"Sometimes, I think you're an act," I said.

Rue giggled. "Little bit."

Hey," she yelled at Rick's back. He slowly rotated around and glared at her. "Can we get some Fried Pickles and two draft beers?" He snorted but wrote it down.

Rue straightened up in her chair. "OK. Now you promised me some stories."

"Once upon a time . . ."

"Back when I was a therapist, I'd smile at that kind of evasion and say, 'It's your money and your time.' Maybe I'll have to start charging you to get you serious."

"And I may have to charge you rent."

She waved that away. "Stories."

"So, you know I'm still committed to my wife Marta."

"Your dead wife Marta?" she said.

I looked at the tight lines around Rue's mouth.

"So this is tough-therapist Rue?"

"Coddling and sugar coating doesn't help anybody. We're here for the truth."

I pointed at the alien poster. "I thought we were here for the beer."

She sat silently and waited.

"And we're here to check out some work supposedly painted by Marta."

"Your dead wife Marta who still paints?"

I glared at her.

"You, of all people, should have no trouble with that."

"I'm not crazy," she said, "just psychically attuned."

"We should get you a T-shirt."

No response.

"It's complicated," I said.

I wanted her to make another smart-ass comment, but she waited me out.

"And it's not easy," I said.

I wanted sympathy, but I got more waiting.

"Or easy to explain."

We sat there. Rick slammed a plate of fried pickles down on the table, and sloshed two mugs of beer all over the table. He wiped up one corner of the table, left the rest in a puddle, and marched away in a huff. Rue made no effort to wipe up the table, just stared at me to see if I could leave it.

I couldn't. I grabbed a handful of napkins out of the dispenser and started mopping up. Rue grabbed a handful out of her side and went to work.

"Oh, thank God," she said. "I was afraid I'd have to either sit here like a good therapist and go crazy letting this mess stare at me or break protocol and clean it up myself, rather than let the client work it out for themselves."

"No, I'm not like that."

She paused and looked at me. "No, you're not."

We both went back to wiping. We piled the wet napkins on the empty table next to us and got a glare from Rick, but we had cleaned up our world.

"I think," I said, "if you're going to understand any of this, you have to understand Marta and my relationship."

Rue gave just the slightest therapist nod.

"I never would have picked the restaurant tonight with Marta around. That was one of the things that she did."

"You complemented each other."

"Yes," I said.

"And now that she's gone, you feel an emptiness in all of those parts of your personality that you gave over to her. You're incomplete."

"Yes."

"And so, you live as though she's still out there, just to fill that emptiness inside?"

I hesitated a long time.

"Yes," I said.

We sat there a long time, Rue waiting for me to talk. Finally, I said, "Or I move on with my life."

CHAPTER 32

Rue and I got up early the next morning and went for a run together. We came to the end of the condo complex and I didn't have to think about which direction to go.

"That way." I pointed to Wave Rock rising to the north of us, looming over the neighborhood like an ancient wave frozen into red stone an instant before it would crest.

We crossed Main Street and made our way uphill through a neighborhood of mixed houses, most new with manicured lawns, others kept in a natural desert. There were artists' houses with colored bottles hanging in trees and strange metal birds staring out from the yard, bankers' houses with BMWs and sprinklers. After a half-mile of uphill running, we came to the trailhead for Wave Rock. Rue kept going up the dirt trail. I caught up with her as she pranced up to a slab of red rock jutting out from under the crest and slowly climbed up with her. We stood there hidden by a pine tree, feeling the sunrise sweep in from our left. I put my arms out and threw my head back.

"Still doubt that there are magical energies here?" she said.

"Energies, yes." I stood there with my eyes closed and the sun on half of my face. I opened my eyes. "The universe hasn't told me about the magic part yet."

She swept her arm from the sun across all the deep red rocks coming to life without saying a word.

"You have a point," I said. I sat down on the rock cross-legged and felt my sweating body shocked by the morning-cold of the rock. Rue sat down and nuzzled against me.

"I feel alive here," I said.

She nodded her head into my shoulder. We exhaled together, laughed nervously at the too-closeness of the moment and stood up quickly.

"We need to get back," I said. "Find some breakfast and get to the gallery by nine. C'mon." I took off lumbering down the hill and she danced past me a minute later. She pushed it down the hill and I was huffing and puffing when I got to the parking lot.

"Wait," I said.

"You wait." She put out a hand. "Give me the keys. I've got to get a shower."

"No, wait." I walked past her to a car two buildings down. It was a black Mercedes. I walked around to the back. A black Mercedes with Oregon plates.

"Dagnabit."

Rue said, "Friends?"

"No, just a couple of guys that want to rob me and kill me."

"Oh, that explains it."

We showered and walked out the door. Ahlstrom and Owl were waiting for us on the sidewalk.

"C'mon," I said to Rue and walked away from them.

They caught up with us, one on each side, and we walked four-abreast across the parking lot.

"Any chance you can leave us alone?" I said.

"None," said Owl.

"Rue," I said, "the pale one here is Martin Ahlstrom, crooked cop turned insurance zealot."

"I was never crooked," said Ahlstrom.

"Did you ever lie to put people in jail?"

"Only if they were perps." He tried to smile at Rue but it just came out scary. "It's important for you to know this, young lady: you are not a perp."

"Thanks," said Rue. To me, she whispered, "I think."

"But bad as the crooked cop is," I said, "he's just the guy who wants to put me in jail. The tall, dark and vicious man beside you wants to torture me until I give him five million dollars."

"The torture is optional," he said.

"His name is Owl," I said. "Probably not his real name, convenient for him when you have to go to the police and identify my body and tell them who did it."

"You have five million dollars?" said Rue.

At the same time, I said, "No," and Owl said, "Yes," and Ahlstrom said, "Not yet."

Rue said, "Clears that up."

Ahlstrom kept bumping up against me.

"We've got something to tell you."

"You're not perps?"

"Even better."

"Oh goody."

Owl said, "Where are we going now?"

"Breakfast. I read about a place called the 'Mom 'n Pop Cafe.' After that, Rue and I have work to do."

"At the Red Rock Gallery?" he said.

I couldn't see any point in pretending. "Yep."

"That's how we found you," said Owl. He beamed over at Ahlstrom. "Or rather, how Martin found you. He really has phenomenal skills as an investigator."

Ahlstrom beamed back, if baring your teeth and chuckling "heh-heh-heh" under your breath can be considered beaming.

"But Owl's the man," he said. "I found the notice about the exhibition. One of Owl's friends got us a whole file on Roger Crosswinds, the owner of the gallery." He leaned in front of

Rue and I to catch Owl's eye. "Paul can see it if he likes, can't he?"

Owl nodded.

We walked into the Mom 'n Pop Cafe, Home of the World's Best Omelets. One wall a mural of Meteor's red rocks, Native American symbols on the other walls. I pulled a vinyl chair out from a wooden table and we all sat down. Rue ordered an avocado, mushroom, spinach and cheese omelet and I ordered a sausage, bacon, tomatoes and cheese. Owl ordered a smoked salmon for him and Ahlstrom to split.

"Your boyfriend here tell you where he hid his wife's body yet?" said Ahlstrom.

I started to say something but the waitress set a coffee cup down in front of me and asked, "Where you people from?"

"Portland," I said.

"Portland. They know real coffee in Portland. Henry, come over here."

A grumpy looking old man shuffled across the floor. Ahlstrom was grinning his skull grin and saying something to Rue but I couldn't hear it for the woman yelling in my ear.

"Henry here is my husband, and he thinks our coffee here is good enough. I say it used to be, but now we've got to step up our game, match the fancy-dancy coffee shop downtown."

I heard Owl telling Rue something about my assaulting a helpless casino employee and hinting that I was a cross-dresser. I tried to say something but couldn't. Over the woman's screeching I heard Rue say, "The universe trusts Paul, and so do I."

"Go on, taste it," the woman said to me, with Henry at her elbow.

I took a sip and tried to listen to what Ahlstrom was saying now.

"Mighty fine coffee," I said, and turned my head.

169

Henry grabbed my shoulder and turned it to him. "It ought to be." He was twice as loud as his wife. "We get the best coffee money can buy and grind it fresh, but that ain't enough for Alice. I say, if folks want fancy-dancy coffee, let them go to the fancy-dancy shop and pay fancy-dancy prices."

I nodded agreement and turned back to the table. Alice grabbed my shoulder and turned me back to her.

"Is it as good as Portland coffee?"

I knew the truth was a mistake.

"Nothing is as good as Portland coffee."

"Ha," she said. "Told you." She snatched up my cup and waved it at Henry, sloshing my precious coffee. "I will not insult this good man with our coffee." She turned to me and beamed. "I will bring you a cup of tea."

I hate tea. I sat there on the verge of tears as my morning coffee walked away from me. I turned back to the table.

"And he and his wife robbed starving reservation women and children of five million dollars."

"I'm sure he had a good reason," said Rue. "Or his late wife did it without his knowledge."

Ahlstrom's turn: "Course, he might not have killed his wife. My theory is that they are in this fraud together, and that she's out there somewhere waiting for him."

Rue opened her mouth to argue and then froze.

"Wait," she said. "Are you saying you've got proof his wife is alive?"

"Probably is," said Ahlstrom. "Or maybe not." He and Owl both nodded.

Rue looked down and stabbed her omelet.

"But that's not the important news," said Ahlstrom.

"The important news is that this great man has opened my eyes and showed me who I was meant to be: a proud, gay man."

He put his arm around Owl. "We are now a very happy couple."

"You just now figured that out?" I said.

He beamed at Rue and I. "Just like you."

I started to say, "no" but Rue was faster and louder.

CHAPTER 33

Rue was quiet walking to the gallery. Ahlstrom and Owl were not.

"Maybe we can run up and see the Grand Canyon while we're here," said Ahlstrom. "Always wanted to see places. Never been out of Portland, till now."

"Much as I'd like to hear about your vacation," I said, "what do you guys know about this gallery?"

"More like a gift shop," said Owl, "until a couple of months ago. Mostly little statues of cowboys and Indians, made in China. Guy who owns the place—guy named Crosswinds—decided to try to upscale things, brought in some local art that he doesn't understand. He's kind of a local grifter, owns a Laundromat and a campground out of town, makes a buck any way he can."

"So what's the Marta connection?"

"My source says Crosswinds claims a guy just walked in with the paintings one day. Claims the guy is a well-known art expert, but he won't give his name. Could just be blowing smoke."

I hesitated.

"Does Crosswinds—or his expert—say when these were painted, or if there's more coming?"

They hesitated.

"You tell us," said Ahlstrom.

Rue stepped ahead of us and threw open the door of the Red Rock Gallery.

"Hello," she said. Nobody answered.

I bumped into her when she froze in the doorway and she jumped when I hit her.

"Sorry," I said.

"No," she said. She pointed at the floor.

An African American man, tall, thin, very dark, almost black, lay on the floor in a pool of darkening red blood. Rue took two quick steps and put her hands on his neck.

She looked up at me with her mouth open and her eyes like a child begging.

"He's dead."

I looked at the man. His arm had three parallel slashes.

Ahlstrom pushed past me.

"Step back, everyone" he said. He pointed to the pool of blood that ran from the body out the door. "You're all standing in evidence." He touched Rue's arm and motioned her back. "This is a crime scene now. Nobody else in the room until we get the police here." He pointed at Owl. "Call it in."

Rue stepped outside and started to cry. I went to her and put my arms around her. In the Bashas' parking lot I saw a black-and-white with an officer putting a sack of groceries in the seat. He studied us for a second and came over.

"Everything all right?" he said. He looked at the pool of blood with our footprints and immediately drew his gun.

"I need you three to put your hands on the window." He motioned at Ahlstrom. "You, sir, come outside."

Ahlstrom reached in his jacket and the cop yelled "Freeze."

Ahlstrom pulled his jacket back and showed his gun and the cop tensed. Ahlstrom reached into his pocket away from the gun and gingerly pulled out his ID.

"Portland PD. Retired."

The cop kept his gun out and talked into his radio. Soon, the lot was buzzing with black-and-whites, two black Caprices and an ambulance. They separated us and detectives got each of our statements. We sat on the sidewalk fifty feet apart, our backs to the walls, and watched.

An older man in jeans, a white uniform shirt and Stetson got out of a jeep and conferred with the detectives. He motioned the four of us together.

"I'm Chief Collins. I understand you four found the body."

We nodded. He looked at me. "And I understand you're the late—your wife painted the artwork in the room."

I nodded.

"But no one knows where she is."

I nodded. He turned to Ahlstrom. "And you're a retired Portland cop who happens to be in Meteor?"

Ahlstrom nodded.

Chief Collins turned to Rue. "And you, young lady, have a drug conviction."

"Grass is not a drug. It is a natural . . ."

He held up his hand. "This is Meteor. Believe me, I've heard it."

He turned to Owl. "Nobody knows who you are."

Owl said nothing.

"And you're all here together from Portland to see Mr. Crosswinds?"

We all nodded.

"Who is not here."

"He was supposed to be here at nine," I said.

"It's almost ten."

Chief Collins ignored us and focused on a car pulling into the parking lot.

"Here he comes now," he said. "OK, I want to talk to him. Then I want to talk to you four some more. Stay close and I'll call you. Don't talk about this until I've talked to you." He turned away from us.

Ahlstrom said to me, "We'll come to your place and hang out there."

"The heck you will," I said.

Chief Collins turned back. "All of you go to the Mom 'n Pop, one block that way. Sit there and wait for me."

CHAPTER 34

I desperately needed a cup of coffee. Henry set one in front of me almost as soon as we sat down in the Mom 'n Pop, the only people there at ten o'clock. Oversized, steaming mug with a smell like heaven and a promise to bring me back to life. I reached for it with both hands.

Alice grabbed first.

"I won't have you insulted by our second rate coffee."

"It's good coffee," I said. "Really, excellent coffee."

"Not for someone from Portland that knows their coffee. I'll bring you a cup when I can serve you something that lives up to your standards. Right now, I'll bring you a nice cup of herbal tea like your girlfriend is having."

I started to ask for warm dishwater instead.

Henry pulled up a chair.

"So are they going to give Simon a medal?" He was grinning. Practically glowing.

Alice ran over and slammed a cup of hot water down in front of me and flipped a tea bag beside it. She pulled up a chair. "Don't you start this without me."

"Well?" said Henry.

"I don't even know who Simon is," I said.

"Simon," said Henry. "Security guard that killed that damned foreigner over at the Red Rock. Wish people in this country had the balls to kill every damned one of these illegal—and that's

176

the word—immigrants sneaking in to steal our jobs and our stuff."

I said, "Oh. We're not supposed to talk about it."

"Well, that ain't stopping the rest of the town," said Alice. "We heard about it before you four had your asses on the concrete waiting for our local Keystone Kops to do their jobs. Or cover it up, more likely. One of their own, that Simon boy, working as a security guard, just starting blasting away and killed hisself an innocent man. Hell, I bet they'll find out the poor dead man didn't even break in, just walking by on the sidewalk and our trigger-happy police gunned him down because he was the wrong color."

"Illegal means you got no rights. Police just can't prove it yet," said Henry.

"This guy Simon wasn't there this morning," said Ahlstrom.

"Cause he's smart." Henry leaned across the table and poked a finger in Ahlstrom's face. "Knows that card-carrying-bleeding-heart-liberals like my wife will probably string him up for doing his job."

Chief Collins walked in holding a battered tan Stetson in his hands. He was a young man with an old man's face: hound-dog eyes and a mouth so turned-down it threatened to fall off his face.

"What do you think of that boy Simon now?" hissed Alice. "You're the one give him a job as a security guard. Look what he done."

"Protected us," said Henry.

Chief Collins stood there so long and still I was afraid he was going to fall asleep on his feet.

"Why don't you two go in the back and leave us alone?"

Henry and Alice looked offended but stood up.

Chief Collins collapsed into Henry's chair.

Ahlstrom said, "Looks like they've already got it all figured out."

"It's a small town. Rumors can fly faster than my men can drive. Right now, half the town's sure of one story, the other half's sure of another one. Facts don't matter much."

He turned to Ahlstrom. "We confirmed that you retired from Portland PD. Recently. Very recently. Your gun will be returned to you as soon as we're done testing it. And we'll have some more questions for you.

"I'd like you to stay in the area, Detective. I'd like all of you to stay in the area."

Ahlstrom nodded. "This guy Simon that they were talking about—you got him in custody?"

Chief Collins gave Ahlstrom a long, flat stare.

"I don't know that I need to have him in custody."

A longer stare, and then a sigh.

"We don't know where Simon is. Simon is the night guard at the gallery. Good kid, hung around the police station, always wanted to be a cop, but he's a little . . . slow. Don't know that he's a suspect. Don't know that someone else didn't do this." He swept each of us with a slow stare. "I'm the one who recommended Simon to the gallery."

He looked at Owl. "Near as we can tell, no one by the name on your driver's license has lived at that address in years."

"Told the detective, I live at the casino."

"The casino doesn't list you as an employee."

"I'm paid informally."

"We'll have some questions for you, too. Formally."

He looked at Rue. "Have you really worked at twelve different jobs in the last year?"

She started counting on her fingers.

"Never mind," he said.

"Mr. McClaron, those paintings in the room where the body

was found, they were done by your wife?"

"That's the claim."

"Your wife who died mysteriously six months ago?"

I didn't say anything.

"The deceased gentleman had no wallet, no ID, no nothing. I find that unusual, don't you, Mr. McClaron?"

"Yes."

"How about you, Detective Ahlstrom? I understand you are—were—a big city homicide detective. You ever had a victim with no identity?"

"No." Ahlstrom brightened. "But I did have a lot of perps who wished I'd never found their identity."

Chief Collins nodded gravely. He reached into his hat and pulled out a white envelope in a plastic evidence bag. He sat it on the table in front of me and covered the return address.

"Is this your wife's handwriting?"

I recognized the scrawl.

"Could be," I said.

He showed no emotion. "Seems pretty distinctive to me. Seems like you ought to recognize it or not."

I didn't say anything.

"Seemed to match your wife's signature on the paintings."

I still didn't say anything.

"There wasn't a letter inside, but just this." He turned the bag over. There was a printed picture of me with my cell number. He flipped it back.

"It was mailed from Phoenix a week ago, about the time your wife's paintings showed up at the gallery." He moved his hand from the return address. "But the return address is from Portland. Do you recognize the address?"

I was having trouble focusing.

"You know it's my home address," I said.

"Yes, sir, I do. But the name is not yours. Is it?"
The name was Paul Fixer.

CHAPTER 35

I had promised to take Rue to check out Oak Creek for her kayaking franchise. We were in The Beast, me trying to make conversation, Rue sitting with her back to me, not talking but staring out the window.

She turned to me and spat out, "So your dead wife sends you mail?"

I stopped talking, too, and we rode in silence.

I just barely made a light and heard car horns wailing behind me.

I looked in the mirror, and saw Owl's black Mercedes run the red light. Saw another black sedan two cars behind Owl pull onto the shoulder around a car and blast through the light, almost hitting a pedestrian.

I jerked The Beast off the road into a convenience store lot and jumped out. Owl pulled in beside me, but the other car tried to keep going. I jumped in front of him and stood in the road until he pulled in.

"Really?" I yelled when he rolled down the window. "You're a Meteor cop who mows down tourists in your unmarked car?"

"I'm not a cop. I'm an ordinary . . ."

". . . An ordinary citizen who has a blue light on his dash and just happens to be following me."

He glared back at me. Ahlstrom was standing beside me.

"Heh-heh-heh," he said.

I was sorry for picking on the guy. Even sorrier that I was

contributing to Ahlstrom's amusement.

"Sorry. Look, I know you're just doing your job. What's your name?"

"Benson."

"Listen, Benson: tell Chief Collins we're going up to Slippery Rock State Park. If you need to follow me, fine. Just stay with me, don't try to kill anyone to prove you're Dirty Harry." I poked a finger at Ahlstrom. "All of you."

I stared them down for a minute and they didn't say anything.

"I'm going inside," I said.

I walked into the store and yelled at the clerk.

"Coffee! And I don't care how crappy it is."

He gave a bored half-wave at a coffee machine in a corner and I realized I had forgotten something. I marched outside and pulled open Rue's door.

I said, "Do you want anything?"

She turned her back and crossed her arms. I slammed the door.

Driving down the road with two cars in tow and hot coffee sliding down my throat, I hoped the day and my mood would get better.

Rue caught me checking the mirror. "Oh they're back there, all right," she said. "Everybody just does what you want them to, don't they? Everything comes so easy for you, doesn't it, with that James Bond confidence and the Robert Redford environmentalist thing and that little boy smile that can charm the pants off a—off a somebody with pants that need to stay on. And you just come along and it's just all so easy to make the same mistakes again."

"Nothing comes easy for me," I said. "My whole life's just a series of stumbles and falls. I was supposed to be a Senator by now, or at least a Congressman. My mother will barely say my name in polite company. My father won't say anything about me except for, 'Well, at least Paul's a good fisherman.' I ain't no fortunate son." I realized I was stealing and I hoped John Fogerty wouldn't mind.

"Paul Fixer. That's exactly what you are, just a fixer. You just shamble through life, and things fix themselves in your path. Poof! There's a beautiful kayak store, a little bit of country peace in the heart of the city. Poof! There's happy people on a river. Paul, Paul, Paul. I am sick of hearing how wonderful you are."

She turned away and then back with a flash.

"You know what, mister? Some people don't need fixing by you. Some of us broken people out here are just happy with the struggle. Not that you would ever know anything about struggling."

"Struggling?" I yelled and stomped on the brakes and the two black cars squealed their tires and car horns went off somewhere. I focused on the road and got back up to speed but realized I was gripping the wheel too hard. I forced myself to lower my voice.

"Struggle? The only woman I ever loved either left me and I don't know why or she's dead or she's missing and I don't know why. I just want to curl up in my bed and watch 'Gunsmoke' but all these crazy things keep happening and I don't know why. I've met the kindest and sexiest woman in my life and I can't even tell her the most important things in my life and I don't know why."

"And you lied to her and told her your wife was dead and now it looks like she's alive."

"I never told you any such thing. I never told anybody anything—"

"You let us think it. Same thing."

We came to the entrance to the Slide Rock State Park and a guy in a wooden booth waited for me to pay the toll.

"Look," I said to Rue. "I don't want to fight, not with you, not with anyone. How about if I commit a random act of kindness? Does that make it all right? Can we get back to being friends?"

I tried to smile at the toll-taker. "I'd like to pay the toll for the next two cars as well as mine."

"The toll is twenty bucks a car."

"Twenty bucks! I thought it was like a dollar or two."

"Twenty bucks. Apiece."

I looked for Rue to take me off the hook but she was staring straight ahead holding back tears. I pulled out sixty dollars and stuck it out the window. Looked in the mirror and realized who I had paid for and almost pulled it back.

Rue and I walked along Oak Creek. I had my shoes off and my pants rolled up, wading in the cold clear water. Rue was walking along the red rock bank next to me.

"Man, look at that," I said. I pointed to a red bluff, green pine trees on top like icing, powder blue sky above.

"Yeah, that's nice," she said.

We came to the slide rock itself, eighty feet of slick rock with the creek flowing over it. Kids were sliding along in the sunshine, squealing and laughing. There was a young woman in a brown uniform sitting on a rock touching up the paint on a sign.

"Excuse me, miss," I said. "Are you a ranger here?"

She laughed. "Ranger, sign painter, convenience store clerk, fixer of skinned knees. Take your pick."

"Looks like a perfect job."

"Everything looks better from the outside. But, yeah, I used to work in a bank in Kansas City. Don't miss it a bit."

"I'll bet. Look, we run a kayak franchise up in Portland, Oregon. Thinking about starting one here."

"Here?" She waved her paint brush at the creek. "This is it, as far as water goes in this area. Great for bouncing down the creek on your butt, but there's not enough water to float a tube, much less a kayak."

I nodded.

"Nearest kayaking is over on the Verde River." She paused. "Of course, Ducky Madness has that franchise sewed up. If you want to work around here, you have to settle for painting signs in the sunshine."

"It was a stupid idea anyway," said Rue. She turned and walked back to the parking lot.

The ride back to Meteor was quiet.

"Look," she said when we got to the edge of town. "We're one week into your six months and I'm going to stick with it. Out of loyalty and commitment and that's all."

I knew I needed to say something but I didn't know what.

"I'm grateful," I said.

She thought about that.

"You should be. You need me whether you know it or not."

"Rue, I think the world of you. I'm sorry I've been awkward about—"

She waved a hand in my face. "Why do guys think everything revolves around sex? It's not that big a deal. If we have sex, it's because it's part of your healing. Nothing more. Look, that's what I'm saying to you." She stared right at me. Her jaw was locked and her eyes were watering. "Sex or no sex, Marta or no Marta, our relationship is purely therapeutic."

That was the moment I wanted anything but therapeutic.

CHAPTER 36

"What on earth is that?" said Rue. She was pointing at the side lot of the The Beacon as we came back into town.

"Sure that 'on earth' applies to that place?" I said. It was supposed to be a joke to break the tension. It didn't.

Rue gestured and I pulled into the lot of the bank next door. The black cars pulled in beside us.

Rue and I didn't wait for them.

Henry met us with a big smile as we walked up to him. "I thought you'd be here." He had four guys wearing jeans and hunting shirts drilling in the Red Planet lot. Each of them carried an automatic rifle.

"You seemed like a good American to me," he said. "I could tell you were just as outraged at that foreign invasion as I was. Get your weapon and join up."

I looked at the army I was asked to join. The oldest was trying to stand on his own even though his walker waited for him at the edge of the lot. The youngest looked like an undersized player from a boys Under 12 soccer team. One of them looked like a high school football lineman gone to seed, complete with a strut and a pot belly. They all wore scowls; they all were white and, right then, I was ashamed to be white.

Rue attacked the football player and grabbed his rifle. He held on.

"Give me that God-damned phallic symbol of death," she screamed. He held on. So did Rue. One strong pull and she and

186

the rifle went clattering to the pavement.

Detective Benson took the rifle away from Rue.

"You can't do that, ma'am." Then he smiled at her. "Though it did look like fun." She didn't smile back.

The chief pulled into the lot and joined us.

Henry turned to the chief. "I got our militia together. Trying to get more from Phoenix, soon as they can get here. Got that radio talk show host spreading the word as loud as he can. We're going to stop this God-damned foreign invasion right here."

The chief said, "Henry, we don't even know if this man was an immigrant, much less illegal."

"You may not, but we do. More aliens coming."

The picture of Henry in full camo, holding a deadly weapon, in the chief's face, with a family of green-skinned aliens waving behind him in the background, was more than I could take.

I went over and tried to help Rue up. She shook my arm off.

"You did this," she said. She jumped up.

"Me? How did I do this?"

"You just—did."

Chief Collins said to Henry, "Make sure that everyone that brings a weapon has a permit and checks in with me. And no discharging your weapons within the city limits."

Henry grinned. "We're going out to Sam's place in the county for rifle drill. Show them, Sam."

The old guy hobbled over to a pile of posters next to his walker and held one up. It was "Pancho," the Chicano sidekick from the old Cisco Kid TV show from the fifties, with target circles printed over him.

"Henry." The chief seemed so tired I felt sorry for him. "The victim wasn't even Hispanic."

"Don't matter. He was a foreigner."

"He was black. We've got a lot of people in Meteor who are

187

black. And Hispanic."

"He was a foreigner, breaking into our country and the gallery to steal our stuff. And you know it."

I tried to help. "Besides," I said. "Pancho and the Cisco Kid were buddies. You know, 'the Cisco Kid, he was a friend of mine.' "

The chief and Henry looked at me like I had been out in the sun too long.

"I need you to come with me," said the chief.

"Why?" I said.

"Need you to finish your work. Need to know if those paintings came from your wife."

I nodded.

"Detective Benson will take you to the gallery."

"I'll walk."

"Detective Benson will take you to the gallery."

It didn't seem to be an argument I was going to win.

"She comes, too." I jerked my chin at Rue. "She's with me."

The chief looked at Rue standing there with her arms crossed, staring off into the distance. A little smile flickered on his face. "You sure?"

"We're with him, too," said Ahlstrom.

"No, they're not," I said.

CHAPTER 37

Ahlstrom and Owl followed us anyway. When we got to the gallery, the detective unlocked the rusty lock on the door and waved us in. I expected him to stop Ahlstrom and Owl, but he waved them in, too.

"Chief said to let them in," he said. "Keep all of you together in the front room."

We went in and Owl took one fast pass around the room, scanning each painting, then started back with the first one.

"Same palette," he said. "Could be the same brushstrokes. Signature looks right."

Owl looked at me. "I made a point of studying your wife's work. I've got to tell you, sometimes it looked like the work of a disturbed woman."

"What do you know about Marta?" I said. "We don't have to listen to you."

"Yeah we do," said the chief. "Want to hear it, whether he's an expert—" He stared at Owl. "—or just blowing more smoke."

I was staring at one painting, trying to focus. There was something in the back of my mind, but I couldn't find it, and I couldn't look for it and talk to Owl at the same time.

I moved to the next painting and he followed.

"You ever notice that all of her paintings have between four and nine scenes in the background?" he said.

"Never counted."

"I have. Wonder why that's so? Maybe a little OCD in there?"

"Must have been hard to live with," said Ahlstrom. "Maybe I've got you wrong. Maybe you did kill her." He chuckled. "Got her to steal you five million dollars, sign up for another five in insurance money, and then do away with the biggest pain in your life."

"You're right," I said. "You have got it wrong."

"Do I? I talked to the cop who filed abuse charges on her."

"That was a misunderstanding."

"Said he saw her whaling away on you with a wooden paint box in the middle of the street, kept hitting you until the box splintered. You just covered up."

"I was all right. She saw a guy in a suit spit on a homeless guy. She went after him and I stopped her and she took it out on me. Marta was all passion and fire. Sometimes it wasn't focused. That's all. The charges were dropped."

"Yeah. After court-mandated counseling. The cop I talked to said he asked you why you didn't just walk away, divorce her. Said you didn't believe in divorce."

"I don't."

"Maybe you believe in murder."

I walked away from him. Owl followed me and I walked over to the other side of the room. The Meteor detective was having a good time watching us.

Rue put her hand on my arm.

"I don't believe you killed Marta," she said. "Whatever else you may be, you are a good man. Maybe the best man I've known."

I tried to laugh but it just came out as a rude noise. "I'm glad somebody thinks so. They don't."

"They don't listen to the universe. The universe practically shouts at anyone who will listen that you are a very good man and a very special man. Ahlstrom doesn't listen to the universe."

"No, he's more of a Joe-Friday-just-the-facts-ma'am kind of

guy. Unless the facts get in the way of a conviction."

Rue snorted. "Facts are great. But unless you listen to the universe to tell you what they mean, then facts are just vicious little gremlins to be twisted and tortured to serve your own evil cause. The tough-guy militia back in The Beacon parking lot think they've got facts. Ahlstrom thinks he's got facts. But they don't have the universe."

I smiled at Rue and our eyes locked. I wanted to tell her how much her faith in me meant. All I could say was, "Thanks."

She broke off and looked at the painting in front of us.

"It really is beautiful," she said.

"How can Owl not see?" I waved at the painting. "How can anyone not love the passion that brings that kind of beauty into the world?"

"No matter what," said Rue.

"No matter what."

Rue stared into the painting. "I can see that."

Owl and Benson came over.

"I'm ready to certify the paintings as genuine," said Owl.

"Good for you. I'm sure the opinion of a two-bit leg-breaker like you will be written up in *Art World and Casino Thug* magazine. Order me a subscription."

Benson was hanging back.

"Chief says he wants a definite yes or no from you before you leave."

"Tell the chief you can't always get what you want."

CHAPTER 38

"I think it's sexist," said Rue.

We were watching *High Noon* and eating veggie pizza in the living room of the condo.

"It's a classic," I said. "Coop standing up to evil with no help from anybody, just doing the right thing because it is the right thing."

"—and the little woman whining about it."

"Well, I mean, Grace Kelly's a Quaker. He's promised to renounce violence for her and become a simple farmer and then on his wedding day he finds out the bad guys are coming on the noon train to kill him."

"—and she says, well, let's just ride out of town. Maybe stop at a nice restaurant for dinner while men are coming to kill you."

"But that's the way people used to think: men had things they did and women had things they did. That was the partnership."

"An unequal partnership. That's what was sexist about it. Because you were a woman you were supposed to act this way, or if you're a guy, that way. Who's to say a woman can't kick ass?"

"Not me. Not to you."

"See, this whole unequal partnership robs them both. He's pretending to be a Quaker, but he's really not. And she—well, she can't even take care of herself without a man." She dragged "man" out to about seven syllables.

"Not a problem you have," I said. It was supposed to be funny.

"No," she said after a long time. "But if I had a partner worth holding on to, I'd keep him strong, not try to make him a half."

"I'm sure you would."

"If I did that sort of thing anymore."

"If."

"Yes." She gave me a look but I was trying not to argue.

"Was it really that bad?" I said. "The old relationship?"

"Yes, it was." She paused. "Hey! I'm the therapist here. We're talking about you."

"I was talking about *High Noon.*"

She grabbed her Tecate and jumped up.

"I'm going to bed. You are not going to transfer your problems onto me."

She stomped up the stairs. I went back to the movie world where the only problems were men with guns trying to kill you. But when I got to the end, to the part where Grace Kelly finally comes to Coop's rescue, it just seemed like too little, too late.

"Where were you when he needed you?" I said as I punched the power button. Went up to bed, but I couldn't sleep. Something about Marta's paintings made me feel achingly lonely.

Rue's door was open as I went by. I stood in the doorway, watching the moonlight stream in through the open window and over her naked body. She looked young and mature, soft and muscled. She turned in her sleep, smiled, and I wondered what the smile meant.

I pulled up the covers and touched her on the shoulder.

"Rue?"

She turned, opened one sleepy eye, and smiled the smile from her dream world.

193

"So now it's time?" she said.

"Yes, I need to talk."

She stretched and her smile grew. "Oh yeah, talk." She looked at my face and her smile fell. "You really do just want to talk. What is wrong with you? You don't just come up to a naked woman, smile that sexy smile and then say you just want to talk."

"You're the one who said nudity was no big deal. Besides, I pulled the covers up."

"Men," she said. "Don't listen when they're supposed to, get it wrong when they do. OK, so I'm the therapist and you're ready to talk now. I suppose that's something. So talk, and then let me go back to bed."

"There's something wrong in the gallery."

"Other than the dead guy and the paintings that may be forgeries or may have been done by a dead person?"

"Yeah. I mean, the paintings themselves."

"Owl said they were genuine."

"Owl knows brushstrokes. I know Marta. Knew Marta. Whatever. Something's wrong and I can't put my finger on it."

"Like your missing half is calling to you?"

I thought about that.

"No." Thought some more. "Look, you're right about that business about Marta and me dividing up one life. And you're right—you and Larry both—that I'm going to have to find what's mine now and not just be a half in search of the other half."

"That's progress," she said.

I nodded.

"So tell me what you're learning about yourself. What do you believe in?"

"I believe in loyalty."

She nodded.

"And I believe in the power of simple human decency for its own sake."

"That," she said, "may be the most appealing thing about you. And it may be the thing that keeps you from moving on."

I sat there in the dark. "Yes," I said.

We sat together and said nothing. Finally, Rue said, "Was there something specific in the gallery that bothered you?"

"Yeah," I said. "Weird as it sounds, there was something specific, but I don't know what it was."

Rue motioned for me to turn around.

"I'm tired of playing nude therapist," she said.

When I looked back she was dressed in black shorts and a black shirt.

"C'mon," she said.

"Where?"

"There's something bothering you in the gallery. So we're going to the gallery."

CHAPTER 39

We went downstairs and peeked out the living room window without turning any lights on.

"There," I said. "Over at the edge of the bank parking lot. Black car."

"Could be." Something shifted inside the car. "Yeah, you're right. That's got to be Meteor PD watching for us. We can't go out that way."

"No back door here."

"But there is a back balcony," she said.

We slid the door open as quietly as we could. She went by me and jumped up on the railing in a single jump, landing like a gymnast on a balance beam. She waved, stepped off and disappeared without a sound.

I had to look over the edge to see if she was all right. She was standing on the ground waving me down. I hooked one leg over the rail, grabbed on with both hands and lowered myself as far as I could go. Turned loose and landed with a crash.

"Shhh," she said.

"Sorry," I said. "It was a long way down—"

She grabbed my head and put her mouth to my ear.

"What part of 'shhh' do you not understand?"

"OK," I said. She clamped a hand over my mouth. Grabbed my head and whispered, "Follow me. And don't fall down."

I followed her out through the development next door, down a back street to the parking lot for the gallery. She crouched behind a dumpster. I crouched behind her.

She turned to me and whispered, "OK. The grocery store is open, but everything else seems empty. No sign of police. We're just going to walk along now like we're making a late night run to the store, turn into the gallery when we get there."

"Just like that?"

"Just like that. Did you get a look at that lock? Take us about two seconds."

"By us, you mean you."

"Keep up," she said.

We walked along the sidewalk, Rue whistling a little tune. When we got to the door, she untied the crime scene tape and slipped a butter knife into the jamb. The door opened and she waved me in.

"Watch the blood," she said.

The lights were on inside and I was glad there were no windows to the outside. I stood away from the blood-stained floor looking at Marta's bright colors on the wall and the darkening blood at my feet.

"This is weird," I said.

"You're just now figuring that out?"

"No, I mean this. Right here, right now. Blood on the floor, death in the air. Paintings that look like they belong upstairs in my house, but I don't recognize any of them."

"Tell me what they remind you of."

I thought. "The first time I saw Marta. Or rather, the time I fell in love with her. I was at an art show in a river park and saw her work. She wasn't even there, but I knew I had to meet her. So I waited for hours until she showed up. We went from there."

"You met her paintings before you met her?" Rue had turned away from the paintings and was looking at me.

"Yeah."

"And that's when you knew?"

197

"Yeah."

She turned back to the paintings. "Probably a good thing you never saw a Van Gogh exhibition. Turn you into a gay necrophiliac, off in Europe, digging up a grave to find your true love."

"Very funny. No, look. How can you not look at the sheer passion here, the ability to create beauty, and not feel something?"

"She's a great artist, I'll grant you that," Rue said. "If this is hers."

"Owl says it is," I said.

"Owl doesn't have your history with Marta and your background with her work. You ever notice that, when you talk about your feelings for Marta, you talk about her painting and her passions, and not about anything between you two?"

I thought about it a long time, walking around looking at the paintings. Rue respected my silence, and walked around in her own circle behind me.

"No," I said. "Well, maybe yes about Marta and me. I don't know. You don't have to have a lot of soft and fuzzy memories to be in love. But you're right about Owl. If we want to know if this is genuine, we've got to look at something objective and not just our own vague feelings."

Rue said nothing.

"Look," I said. "Owl's right. The brushstrokes are right. The palette's right."

"You sound like a man," said Rue, "trying to convince himself of something."

"I'm just trying to figure out what's real and what is not."

"And you think listening to other people is the way to do that?" she said.

"Sometimes, other people are right. Let's go home. Looking at these is just making me feel empty."

I took a step toward the door and stopped.

"That's it," I said.

Rue stood beside me and waited. I turned back around and scanned the paintings.

"That's it, don't you see?" I pointed at each painting one by one. "No, no, no, no, no."

Rue still waited.

"The backgrounds on Marta's paintings all told stories. That's what I would stare at for hours, trying to find the stories." I stepped up to one painting. "Look at this. What do you see, in the background?"

"Scenery. Different mountains and rocks from Arizona."

"Scenery! Marta would never have painted this. She could never resist the chance to tell a story, make a point, get her ideas across. This isn't her."

I turned to Rue.

"Marta isn't here."

CHAPTER 40

We pushed a couple of tables together at the Mom 'n Pop to make room for Rue and me, Ahlstrom and Owl and Benson. As far as I could tell, we were the only ones in the place paying for our meals. Alice hovered over the table, filling cups from a glass carafe.

"Henry won't let me charge those yahoos." She waved the pot over at the loud men milling around on one side. "And I won't charge my own." She waved it over at a group of mostly middle-aged women painting signs and eating breakfast on the other side.

"Any trouble?" I asked.

"Not from mine," she said.

She waved the pot over my cup and then pulled it away.

"Whoopsie. I nearly forgot about you."

She took the pot and walked away from me.

Chief Collins walked in and dropped his hat on the table in front of me.

"Move over," he said. He pulled up a chair and wedged between Ahlstrom and me, which suited me fine. "Make room for these guys, too." We pulled over another table and two Meteor cops joined us.

"I blame all this on you," he said to me.

"Me?"

"You and your wife and her paintings. Nothing worth steal-ing in that gallery until her paintings mysteriously appeared, followed by you, who also mysteriously appeared, just before the equally mysterious dead body appeared. I can't talk to your wife, I can't talk to the victim, and I can't even talk to Simon. All I've got is you."

"Any progress, Chief," said Ahlstrom, "on finding Simon?"

"None. He lives with his mother, and she hasn't seen him. He doesn't drive. Doesn't do much but go to work, go home and watch football reruns, and hang around the police station."

"Any history of taking off?" said Ahlstrom.

"I don't think he's ever left the county. He's a good kid, even if he wasn't bright enough to pass the police exam. I'm the one who got him the job at the gallery. Told Crosswinds not to let him have a gun, but who knows? This is Arizona, easy to get a gun. If you buy a gun and cigarettes at a convenience store, they'll make you show ID for the tobacco and ignore the gun."

Ahlstrom said, "Is Simon your suspect?"

The chief waved his hands at me. "Along with this guy. Personally, I can't imagine Simon shooting anyone, let alone shooting them outside and then dragging them into the store. But yes, he has to be a suspect."

Alice banged a plate down in front of the chief.

The chief nodded thanks. "So either we lynch a good man to satisfy half the town." He poured syrup on his pancakes, took his time setting the pitcher down and looked straight at me. "Or we find the real killer." He waited for me to say something but I didn't. "I'm betting we catch the real killer, Mr. McClaron." He cut a bite of pancakes and held it up. "Again, Mr. McClaron, don't leave town."

I nodded. "There's one piece of information you need to know, Chief. Those paintings were not done by Marta."

The chief chewed slowly and pointed his fork at Owl. "He says they were."

"He's wrong."

Owl said, "The technique is hers and the signatures appear genuine. Chief, we believe Ms. Strauss-McClaron is alive. And Mr. McClaron here has reasons to pretend she's dead."

The chief looked at Owl. "And I have reasons to wonder about you, too. These people call you 'Owl.' Your driver's license says Jeffrey Petersen. I understand his interest in this case," he pointed the fork at Ahlstrom, "as an insurance investigator. But I don't understand yours."

Ahlstrom put his hand on Owl's. "We're friends."

The chief didn't react.

Owl pulled his hand away. "I'm also an art expert." He looked at me. "I don't appreciate having my judgment impugned. The paintings are genuine."

The chief smiled. "It looks like nobody here likes you very much, Mr. McClaron."

"I do," said Rue.

"Except your girlfriend," said the chief.

"She's not my girlfriend," I said.

"Looks like nobody around you is who they appear to be."

The chief looked past me and yelled, "Hey."

I looked and saw the high school football player militiaman just inside the front door, holding an AK47. He gave the chief a "Who me?" look.

"Yeah, you, Claude," said the chief. "Take that thing back to your truck. Lock it up."

The chief gave the militiamen a tired look. "Fellows, you need to cool down. We haven't even proved that the victim had a name. What makes you think you know he was illegal?"

Henry said, "Crosswinds. Owner of the gallery told us he bet the guy was just an illegal, thieving immigrant. We'll probably never know his real name."

The chief said, "Crosswinds told us he had never seen the man before."

I started to say something but Rue interrupted.

"Hey," she said. "We need to go to the gallery."

The chief turned to Rue.

"Why is that, miss?"

"Because. Well, because we need to know for sure who painted the artwork in the gallery. We need to get Mr. Mc-Claron and Mr. Owl in there together, let them figure it out together while we watch them."

The chief thought about it.

"Sounds like a good idea." He stood up and the two cops and Detective Benson stood up, too. "Let's go."

A guy who looked like a ZZ Top member stood up and motioned for the other men.

"We're coming, too," he said.

From across the room, Alice said, "You're not going to leave us out."

CHAPTER 41

So the chief organized us all in the parking lot of the Mom 'n Pop.

"All right, you four go first," he said to us. "Benson, you stay with them. Call down to the station and get the keys down to the gallery so we can get in."

I looked at Rue but she showed nothing.

"Play along," she said out of the corner of her mouth.

"You watch too much TV," I said.

The four of us, followed by the crowd, slowly snaked down Main Street, in and out of parking lots, traffic slowing beside us. After ten minutes, we came to the gallery. A uniformed officer was waiting at the door.

"Looks like the lock was jimmied," he said.

Detective Benson shrugged and pushed the door open. All of us followed him in and the chief stood in the doorway.

Rue pulled out her phone and took a close up of one picture.

"Are you sure about this?" I whispered.

"Play along," she said again.

Owl stepped into the center of the room.

"Gentlemen, we really need to get several of Ms. Strauss-McClaron's paintings in here and do a thorough comparison. But doing the next best thing and relying on memory and pictures on my computer, I can show you several things. One, look at the signatures. If you compare them, they appear to be real. Second, the palette—the choice of colors—is distinctive. In fact, it is unique. No other artist used quite the dramatic contrast of dark and bright as Strauss-McClaron. No one. Many experts consider it garish and overly dramatic."

He looked at me for a reaction but I gave him nothing.

"Her brush strokes are crude on the broad sweep of the painting, mixed with almost an obsessiveness in the unnecessary details she felt compelled to add behind her paintings. It's a unique style, and—while it is popular right now—not a style that most art experts believe will hold up with time.

"And—for that reason—" he turned back to me "—she is the only one who painted in this style. And appears to still be painting in this style, which should be of interest to Mr. McClaron." He turned to the chief. "Probably painting somewhere near here, which may be of interest to you."

He stepped back and motioned for me to take the floor.

"Much of what Mr.—ah—Owl says is true," I said. "The technique is Marta's. Even the signature looks like hers, although that could be faked.

"Chief, there's a great book by a man named Nathan Stevenson called *Behind the Canvas.* Your detectives need to get a copy. As long as people just saw only what Owl sees, Marta's paintings never sold. To anyone. She was immensely unpopular. People would look at her works and cringe. Then something changed."

"Yeah," said Ahlstrom. "You and she faked her death to get rich and people bought her paintings because they felt sorry for the dead girl." He paused and waited until I started to say something before he interrupted me.

"Or you killed her," he said.

"He didn't kill her," said Owl. "She's out there."

"Oh, you're just so sure of yourself," said Ahlstrom.

"Sure of some things." They beamed at each other.

"Actually, the interest started before her disappearance," I said. "The book I mentioned took several of her paintings and broke down the stories behind the backgrounds, including one painting that has at least two interpretations of the stories. People started coming in to the gallery, spending hours rather than minutes with her paintings. When they left, they sounded like people leaving a movie, arguing, 'Did you see that part?' or 'Why did this character react this way?' That was Marta. She saw the world so intensely and with so much passion that, even in small details, the stories she saw demanded to be told. Look at these paintings, and behind the surface you'll just find scenery. No stories. No pain. No emotion. Marta was incapable of painting these."

Rue grabbed me and pulled me aside.

"Excuse me," I smiled to the crowd. The chief was watching me.

"We need to get out of here," she said.

"What? You were the one who wanted this."

"Now I've got what I want here. The universe is calling us somewhere else."

I looked at her and saw that she was serious. Or the universe was serious. I stepped back.

"Of course, I could be wrong," I said. "Owl is right, we need to get some paintings and experts in here and do a real comparison."

"Well, I guess we're done here." Rue took my arm and rubbed up against me. "And now my boyfriend and I need to get out of here. Have you got a bookstore nearby?"

"Dharma House Books," said Henry. "Down the street. We'll come with you."

"No," said Rue.

"Yes," said Alice. "All of us."

Rue fidgeted, turned red. She went over to Alice and whispered in her ear. They whispered back and forth. Alice finally smiled and put her hands on her hips and stood in the door.

"They're going," she said. "Alone."

CHAPTER 42

"What did you say to her?" I said.

We were walking fast across the parking lot, Rue's eyes straight ahead, me looking back at a deputy trying to talk his way past Alice and having no luck.

Rue said something, but I had fallen behind and had to catch up.

"What?" I said.

Rue shouted, "I said I needed a sex book. Techniques and such." A mother with two toddlers gave Rue a dirty look but we kept going.

"What?" I said. "How could she believe that? You're a normal, healthy woman. No one would believe you'd need help with that sort of thing."

"Told her it was for you."

"Oh," I said.

"Sorry." She took my arm. "It was the only thing I could think of to get them to leave us alone. Worked."

We walked on a little.

"I don't, you know," I said. "Need a book."

"Can't prove it by me," she said.

"Anyway, I know that can't be it," I said. "So what's the big idea?"

"You don't trust me?" she said.

Someone bumped me from behind and I turned and saw the high school linebacker/militiaman.

"Claude," I said. "How'd you get past Alice?"

"Takes more than an old lady to stop me," he said.

Rue turned and glared at him.

Claude said, "Plus she said I wouldn't understand no ways."

"Neither do I," I said.

"Whatever it is, I'm going to put a stop to it. Just want you to know my hands aren't tied like the police."

"What if what we're doing is not illegal?" I said.

"I'll be the judge of that." His voice dropped an octave.

The woman behind the desk at Dharma House Books shook herself when we came in and gave us a dirty look for disturbing her nap.

"Go to the back." Rue whispered and pointed to a rack of maps. "Get every topographical map you can find for Arizona."

I walked back and Claude followed.

"What kind of maps would you need," I asked him, "for hunting around here?"

He drew himself up.

"Real man don't need no map."

I grabbed maps for Yavapai County, Coconino County, and a couple more.

I took them to the front. The clerk was grinning at Rue and shoving books in a bag so Claude and I couldn't see. Claude's eyes lit up.

"I need to see those, ma'am. I represent the Coconino County militia."

Rue laughed at him, but Claude yanked the bag away and turned it over on the counter. A stack of hot pink books with naked people on the covers tumbled out. Claude stared at the top one until it dawned on him what the couple on the cover were doing. He turned red and glared at me.

"Real man don't need this neither."

CHAPTER 43

Every step of the walk home, the bag of scx books and maps bumped against my leg. Every step, Rue rubbed against my other leg. Every step, my mind had a new image of what Rue was going to do with sex manuals, maps, and me.

As soon as the condo door closed, Rue ran up the stairs to the bedroom and I followed her with my bag. She threw off her blouse.

"I'm going to get a quick shower. You spread those maps out on the bed."

I looked at Rue, topless. I was helpless and eager.

"Should I?" I opened the top button of my shirt and put my hands on the second button.

"Men," she snorted. She put her hands on her hips. "Why do you think everything is about sex? Besides, even if I said, 'Alright, let's get this therapy started,' you'd get a case of the guilts and start chattering about how Marta had all the passion. No. Keep your clothes on. And clear off the bed." She looked at me. "For work."

Then she was gone and I was standing there with a tent in my pants and a bed full of maps.

Rue came out, dripping and naked and excited.

"Where's my phone?"

I pointed at her. "Can you do something about—that?"

She smiled, just to herself and just for a second, before she said, "Oh, for crying out loud, it's just a human body." She did smile at me. "See, you've even got me cursing like you now."

She ran into the next room and came back with a pair of jeans on but still no shirt.

"Give me one of your fishing shirts," she said. She reached into the closet and pulled out my favorite shirt, blue check with insect repellant built in and half a dozen pockets.

"Don't—I mean, don't stretch my shirt out."

She tucked the shirt in and giggled. The shirt hung on her like a tent.

"I'm not one of those girls who's built like that. You obviously haven't been paying attention."

"I obviously have."

She beamed and then wiped the smile off.

"We've got work to do." She pulled out her cell and played with it a minute. "Look at this painting."

I looked. "Yeah. One of the not-Marta paintings from the gallery."

"Look at where it's hanging, and hold that thought."

She yanked the phone away, brushed her fingers across its face and handed it back to me.

"That's the same wall, taken the night we first went to the gallery. Before the man was killed."

I looked at it and looked at Rue. She and the universe had figured something out.

"This painting's not there," I said.

"The dead man—truly, the victim—wasn't breaking in to steal anything. He was breaking in to hang one of his own paintings."

I pushed the phone at her.

"How do you get back to his painting on this thing?"

She caressed the phone.

"Here."

I looked. "A painting that looked so much like the Marta

paintings that we never noticed. Same palette. Same styles."

"Yeah. Take a look at the background."

"Scenery," I said. "Not stories, like Marta. Wait, I've seen that rock in another one of the paintings."

"Yeah," she said. "I'll bet most of these show up in one of the other paintings or another. He painted what he had at hand. And look at the signature."

Instead of Marta, it read, "Jean-Paul Chrisafis."

"French," said Rue.

"Or a former French colony," I said. "Like Leongo."

"Well, maybe," she said. "But look at the important part. We figure out where these scenes are, and we know where this was painted. Maybe where all of them were painted."

I looked at the tiny picture on her camera. I picked up a notebook I keep next to my bed and sketched a red mesa from the phone, ripped the page out and handed it to Rue.

"You're looking for this."

"On it." She leaned over the bed and tried to find the mesa on a map.

I saw a distinctive mountain with two spires like a church. Made myself a sketch and went to work looking for it.

We were getting in each other's way, sliding our little pieces of paper over the maps and finding no place where the papers fit. But, like a two person game of Twister, every time we slid the papers we found a new way our bodies would fit together. I was sweating even in the cool room.

I pulled back. "This is getting us nowhere. Let's think about this."

Rue was sweating, too. We sat there on the bed facing each other across the maps.

"Yeah," she said.

"The red rocks are concentrated in a small area around Sedona and Meteor. But we can't find anything that looks like either of our two drawings."

"So let's make some more drawings."

"Yeah. But let me look through all of the paintings, concentrate on the things that show up more than once."

She opened up my computer. "I'm just going to look at pictures of the area, see if anything jumps out at me."

We worked and muttered for a few minutes.

"See what you can come up with on this one," I pointed at a detail on the phone. "Seems to be in a lot of the paintings. It's the only one with buildings, too."

She draped herself over my shoulder and looked at the phone. "Looks like old buildings, too. See, look at that big one, up near the top? Like an old hotel or something. The mountain it's on looks more rounded than what you see around here, too." She leaned over me so she could see my face. "Could be that these are just scenes taken from a lot of different places."

"Then we're out of luck."

"The universe would never leave us out of luck."

"Well, tell the universe to find us something."

She and the universe went back to the computer.

"Hey, hey, hey," she said after a minute. She reached over and snatched the phone out of my hands, held it up to the screen.

"Jerome, Arizona." She beamed. "Say 'thank you, Miss Universe.' "

I looked at the screen.

"Thank you, Miss Universe."

CHAPTER 44

Rue came out of the convenience store with her arms piled with water bottles, crackers, batteries and lighters.

"How can they not have bags?" she fumed.

I stopped pumping gas for a minute. Opened the passenger door and held it while she dumped her load on the seat.

She put my backpack on the floor of The Beast and started stuffing things in. Paused and looked at the sky: clear, hot, the sun right over our heads. Still plenty of daylight left in the day. I finished pumping and we climbed in.

As we pulled out of the convenience store lot, Rue said, "At least we got away without the twins."

"Yeah." I motioned at an off-road truck too shiny and new to have ever been off-road, pulled onto the side of the road a quarter mile past the store. "But we picked up Claude."

As we went by, I waved but he looked away like he hadn't seen us.

"Pull over," said Rue. "I got a message for him."

"Later," I said. "We need to get up there while we have daylight. He's harmless."

"Yeah, well, if he's got no bite then I wish he'd stop barking. Loudmouths like him bug me."

"Maybe the universe tells him to act that way."

"No, and that's what bothers me. And that's the difference between you and guys like him. You can make one little statement and cut to the quick. Because you are grounded in the universe. Deep in your soul there's something that feels a sense of right and wrong and beauty and decency and you feel your place in something much bigger than yourself."

"I thought I just liked old movies."

"No, really, and that's the thing. Because you've got that connection, got it so strong, got it every minute, you don't need to brag about it. Guys like Claude say and do one mean thing after another because they don't feel that connection to anything, don't know who they are, and have to scream and strut to cover up. I understand it, but it doesn't change the mean things they can do. Guys like him need their own kind of therapy."

I smiled. "You going to take him on as a client?"

"One at a time. Besides, I don't think I could take six minutes with Claude, let alone six months."

"How about you? Have you been one with the universe since you were born?"

Her mouth got tense. "The universe and I have a more complicated relationship. I struggle. She loves me; she hates me. She's there in everything I see, and then sometimes I feel so all alone, like she's gone away and will never come back for me."

"You make it look effortless."

"It's not," she said. "I've got a mean streak a mile wide sometimes."

I didn't say anything.

"Faith," she said. "That's what I believe in. When your head tells you things make no sense, your heart can carry you on faith. And when your heart is sick and ready to give up, your head can tell you to keep the faith no matter what. The universe comes and goes, but faith abides."

"Maybe that's it," I said. "There's a light that comes through you. I used to think it was just a simple unshakeable naive belief. I can see that it's something you work at. Makes it more special."

She was smiling at me and she looked so fragile and childlike and precious that I stared and she blushed and wiped her smile off.

"Watch the road, mister."

She fished the map off of the floor and studied it. It was covered with our drawings of the landmarks we had found in the paintings. There was a big circle in the middle of them.

"Looks like, after we leave Jerome, we follow a Park Service road and then just a fire trail or two. Hard to say how fast we can go on those, or how much blind searching we'll have to do."

"Count on maybe five miles an hour," I said.

Rue said, "The problem is figuring the miles. Once you're up in the hills, what looks like a mile on the map can become ten. Or more. Maybe we should just go back and tell the chief, let him handle it."

"There may be things I want to find for myself," I said.

"Just saying this may not be easy."

"Faith."

Rue was quiet a long time.

"Think Marta will be there?"

I didn't say anything for a while.

"Think she's still alive?" I said to Rue.

"Do you?"

A mile went by and we didn't speak.

I said, "The thing is this: if I think she's alive—if I act like she's alive—it will kill her. Or it will hurt an important part of her. If she's alive."

"So that's what you can't talk about?"

"Yes."

Another mile went by.

Rue said, "If you have to act like she's dead, regardless, then I will, too."

I nodded.

"But if I do see her," said Rue, "how should I act?"

"Carefully."

"So if she's alive, she's dead, and she's also dangerous?"

"See, Marta's just very passionate and doesn't always think . . ."

Rue looked out the window. "There's more than one way to be passionate, if you haven't noticed."

The Beast struggled as we climbed the hill up to Jerome. Jerome was a cluster of semi-restored historic buildings clinging to the side of a dry hill miles away from anything else. A booming mining town from the 1880s when a New York paper called it "the wickedest town in the West," until the 1950s when the copper ran out, Jerome is now a small tourist ghost town with a permanent smattering of artists, hermits and drifters who came in with motorcycle clubs and decided to stay. I parked outside an Old West bar that looked like someone had started restoring it and given up. The street was empty except for a family in Michigan t-shirts consulting a map, and a local guy, unshaven and wearing a black leather vest and no shirt, rocking back on a cane chair trying to figure a way to ensure that some of the Michigan money stayed in Jerome.

We went inside the bar. A ceiling fan stirred the dusty air, but nothing else moved.

"Hello," I called out. "Anybody home?"

A small bald man with a handlebar mustache and tattoo sleeves on his arm took one step in from the back and no more.

"Yeah?" He seemed to have better things to do.

"You open??"

"Well, of course I'm open. Why the hell do you think I'd be here if I wasn't open?"

"Sorry. No offense. What you got on draft?"

"Nothing. Not much in bottles, either." He ripped open a cooler behind the bar and started slamming cans and an occasional bottle on the bar. "Stop me when something looks good."

I grabbed a can of Tecate. Rue took a Coors. He grunted and shoved the others back.

"Ten bucks," he said.

I raised my eyebrows.

"Take it or leave it. Cottonwood's a long ways away."

I fished out a bill.

"Got anything to eat?"

"What you want? Don't have filet mignon."

"How about a burger and fries?"

He looked like I had asked him for a kidney, but he drug himself around the bar and out onto the street.

"Hey, Steve," he yelled.

After a minute there was a noise from a doorway across the street.

"Cook me up a burger and fries, will you?" He looked back at Rue.

"I'm a vegetarian," she said.

"Well, ain't that good for you?" he said. Yelled back, "Cook up one of those mushroom sandwiches you make for the fancy folks, too." He turned back to Rue. "If you don't mind listening to the cries of the poor downtrodden Momma Mushroom as Steve butchers her baby for your amusement."

"I can stand it."

He came back in and picked up a dirty rag and stood there shoving a little pile of dust from one end of the bar and back like a cat toying with a mouse. But he kept his eyes on us.

I tried smiling. "We're looking for some people who live up in the hills off the forest road to the north of town."

"Nobody lives up there."

"Well, if they did."

"They wouldn't. That's National Forest. The federal government says you can hike there, go tra-la-la-ing along picking daisies and singing 'Kumbaya,' but you can't do anything useful like hunt or run cattle or live there."

"But if someone did live there."

He leaned over and waved the rag in my face.

"If they did live there, they would be illegal and they would shoot anyone who came looking for them. Got it?"

"Got it."

Steve came in with our food on paper plates.

"Fifty dollars," he said.

I looked at the dried-up roll on my plate. "I'll give you twenty. Nineteen of it is a tip."

He took the bill and walked out.

The guy behind the bar said, "I'm going in the back and watch golf. Tiger's on a roll and I don't want to miss it. Try not to steal anything."

I looked around and couldn't see anything to steal. Rue and I looked at each other, giggled, and ate.

She looked out the window and saw Claude's truck parked down the street.

"Hey," she yelled. The guy came out.

"Yeah?"

"You got a soda back there?"

He reached in and slammed a can down on the counter.

Rue picked up the can and headed out. I put down a five and followed. By the time I got there, she was rapping on Claude's window with the can. He rolled down the window and air-conditioned air and the sound of a metal band blasted out onto the dry street.

Rue slammed the can in. "We're going up that road. Try to keep up."

CHAPTER 45

Claude took Rue as seriously as she took the universe. The boy gave up on stealth and rode my bumper as we bounced along the gravel road.

"Tell your boy toy to give us a little more room," I said to Rue.

"He's not mine," said Rue.

"You fed him."

"I threw a can at him."

"You were flirting," I said.

She snorted at the same time Claude smashed into our rear. The Beast jumped and skittered but stayed on the narrow gravel. Rue and I got out. Claude was waiting for us, waving an AK47 in one hand like Schwarzenegger or Stallone.

"Put two hands on that thing, son," I said. "And don't point it at us." I looked at the crumpled back of The Beast. "For crying out loud."

"You're under arrest," he said.

"Since when are you police?"

"Don't have to be. I'm an American. Chief told you not to leave town. I'm taking you in, tell him I caught you trying to escape."

I put my hand on a dangling piece of sheet metal and it ripped off in my hand. I waved it at him and he aimed the rifle at me.

"Is this your idea of a Wild West standoff? Your gun against my scrap metal?"

I pointed it at him.

"Bang, you're dead. C'mon. This isn't Rambo or Cops and Robbers. We've got an errand out here. Call the chief, tell him we'll be back tonight or tomorrow. Also tell him we're filing charges on you for this."

I went over and bent down over The Beast's tailgate. "Looks like a couple of thousand dollars in damages."

"Shit. Fix it with a crowbar and a tub of Bondo, if you were a real man. I ain't paying for what you brought on to yourself. Taking you in, and then I'm coming back with Henry and the rest to clean out that nest of the invaders."

"Sure you will." I looked back at The Beast. "Twenty years of driving in Portland traffic, and not a scratch. This is the only thing that I've had with me for twenty years. I took care of it, and now one moment, one yahoo."

Rue said, "Is it drivable?"

"Sure. Take more than this boy to stop The Beast."

"We'll get her fixed, Paul. Let's get going. Burning daylight."

She pulled open her door.

"Stop right there." Claude pointed the AK47 at Rue.

"Shoot me." She slammed the door and I followed.

I leaned out the window. "Twenty years," I said, cranking the engine. I leaned out and yelled at Claude, "This is not Rambo, son, just an ordinary drive in the woods."

The park road turned into a dirt fire trail clinging to the side of the hill, a thousand foot drop to the valley below. I stayed as far away from the edge as I could.

The trail widened into a long meadow. Claude gunned his truck around us and pointed the AK47 out the passenger window at me.

"Pull over," he said.

He was bouncing inches from my window.

"Ease up, dang it," I said.

Rue shot him a bird.

He yelled at her and his truck jerked. The gun exploded in my ear and shattered the windshield in front of me. Glass flew everywhere and my head rang like a bell and I fought to keep The Beast steady. Through the raining glass, I saw Claude, panicked and fighting to get control of his gun or his truck.

He got neither.

The big metal rack on the front of his truck locked onto the rear of The Beast and suddenly we were now one big chunk of metal and flesh, spinning out of control to the edge. I wrestled the wheel but we were sideways in a choking cloud of red dust.

My eyes grabbed onto Rue. For an instant, she was the one solid center in a crazy world spinning around her. But she was screaming for me to help her, and there was nothing I could do.

The ground disappeared and The Beast tilted at a crazy angle. We stopped. Rue and I looked at each other and everything froze for a moment.

The Beast shifted and made sounds like a baby crying.

"Going fast," I said. I looked out my window and saw dirt.

"This way. Move fast but smooth."

I cracked the door open, put one foot out and felt solid ground. Slid out and grabbed back for Rue.

"Easy," I said. She slid across and The Beast let out a moan and started sliding over the edge.

"Wait," she said. She reached back and grabbed my backpack.

"Dang it, Rue." I snatched her and the backpack out and caught them in one motion. We stood there together on solid ground feet from the edge and held each other like it was forever.

"Tell your universe I will be forever grateful," I said.

She was starting to cry when we heard Claude.

"Help me, mister."

The trucks made another groan and The Beast slipped a little farther over the edge, hung up on a rock and teetered there moaning. His truck was on solid ground for the moment, but the two vehicles were locked.

"Help me, mister," he said again. He yanked on his seat belt but it was stuck and his eyes were crazy-scared and he kept rocking harder and harder.

"Hold still," I jumped over and grabbed his arms. "Settle down. Don't move."

I let go of his arms and he grabbed the seat belt and went back to jerking violently and The Beast screeched louder and the tires on his truck started to slide in the dirt and I had to crab-walk sideways to stay with him.

I grabbed his arms again and held them still. Rue eased in. "Get away, Rue. This thing's going."

"Like hell I will," she said. Rue stroked his cheek and turned his face to her.

"Look at me." She forced a smile at him. "Be calm. Look at me. Look only at me."

She kept talking and smiling and I slid my hands away and Claude's arms stayed still. I grabbed a hunting knife off the floor and sliced the straps and stepped back.

"OK," said Rue.

She stepped back and held out her arms. "Step out of the truck gently and come to me."

The trucks shifted again. The front wheel of his truck lifted off the ground and Claude hesitated.

"Come to me," said Rue, with a big Mamma-bear smile.

The trucks shifted again and picked up momentum to the edge. I grabbed his arm and yanked. He fought me, reached back into the truck and grabbed his AK47. I pulled him and the rifle onto the ground away from the trucks. He came up for air in the cloud of dust and gave Rue a cocky action-hero smile.

"Really?" Rue's smile was gone, she was covered with red

dust and she looked like something from a dark corner of hell. "You are one step from taking us all off a mountain, we save your life and this—this is all you can think of?"

She grabbed the barrel of the rifle in both hands like a baseball bat, wound up and knocked Claude across the road away from the trucks.

"This, and the kind of tough-guy thinking that goes with this, is what got us here. I hate it." She wound up again and hurled the rifle off the mountain.

The trucks shifted again with a terrible scream and broke over the edge. Rue and I stood in the cloud of dust and watched them spinning away in the air. Rue was still breathing hard and her hands were clenching.

I heard Claude crying on the ground behind us. I watched my only reliable companion for twenty years break herself into pieces on the rocks.

Rue sat down in the middle of the road and closed her eyes to meditate.

"The universe doesn't like me when I get like this."

CHAPTER 46

I stood in the middle of the dirt road with Rue communing with the universe on one side of me and an overgrown boy crying on the other. At the bottom of the mountain was a truck I had lavished my whole adult life on, now just a pile of broken metal. We were miles away from anything.

I picked up my backpack and sat down. We had a half-dozen water bottles and a handful of granola bars. I opened my cell phone and turned it on. No bars.

I pulled out the map and sat down on the ground with it in front of me and started making marks. I didn't like what I saw.

Rue put her hand on my shoulder.

"You and the universe back on speaking terms?"

"Yeah. Thanks for hanging in with me when I get . . . like that."

"Looked pretty good to me. Wonder if that swing will make the Sports Center highlights."

She smiled, one of those first-smiles-back-from-anger smiles and I reached up and put my arm around her waist.

"OK," she said. "Now that we've dealt with that important matter of my ego, how about something insignificant like our survival?"

I ran my fingers on the map.

"I figure we're about here. Miles away from Jerome. And it's getting dark. No way we can make it back before we lose the light.

"But look. We're on the edge of the circle where we think the paintings were done. We can push on, hope to find somebody up there. If not, there's a fire tower here," I jabbed the map. "We can make it there. There should be supplies, maybe even cell coverage."

Rue said, "Sounds like the smart play would be to head back to Jerome, get as far as we can today. Get back tomorrow sometime."

I didn't say anything.

"But you want to get up there, maybe find Marta, who may have died six months ago, standing at an easel waiting for you."

"No. I don't think Marta's there anymore. Think she taught the technique and moved on."

We stood there with Rue's hand on my shoulder and my arm around her.

"Thought about something else. I'm not looking for Marta. I'm looking for answers."

She kissed me on the head.

"Then let's go find answers."

Claude was standing up now, rubbing the tears away with a big hand.

"I want to go home now."

I nodded. "Claude, it's a long ways down the road that way back to Jerome. We think there may be some people up this way. We're going up this way and take our chances."

"I want to go home."

"Your call. We can give you some of the water, a couple of granola bars. You go that way. We go this way. Whoever gets help first sends help for the other."

"Yeah. I want my share."

Without pointing out that it was a share of our stuff, I divided the supplies up. I pulled the pack onto my back.

"Good luck," I said to Claude. To Rue, "Let's get going."

"Burning daylight," she said.

We took a few steps and she looked back. Claude was still standing in the road.

"I've never been in the woods without my four-wheeler and my gun. There's bears and rattlesnakes here, you know."

"We know," said Rue. "Go on, you'll be all right. Stick to the road. Sleep when it gets dark. You'll get there sometime tomorrow."

"I have to sleep out here?"

"You'll be fine." She turned back and I followed her. In a few steps, we heard heavy breathing behind us.

"Take me with you."

I could see Rue's mouth tighten and I thought she was going to chase him away like a stray dog. Instead, she softened.

"C'mon."

"Probably better for you," said Claude, "if you have me along to protect you."

"Yeah, that's it," I said.

We made another mile before we came to a ledge just off the path.

"Looks like a Motel Six to me," I said, dropping the pack.

"Wish I had my rifle," said Claude. "Bring down a deer for dinner."

"Yeah, well, check under there for rattlesnakes. Kill one of those, and we can at least have meat for dinner." I looked at Rue. "At least, some of us can."

"You kill a rattlesnake hiding in what's going to be my home for the night, and I'll eat him raw."

"You might."

Claude looked horrified. "I'm not going in there without a gun."

I found a stick. "Take this. Think of it as a first generation gun."

He went in and rattled the stick around the rocks, I think with his eyes closed. Rue dumped a load of sticks and pine cones in front of the ledge for a fire.

"Look." I pointed out past where the path dropped off to nothing.

"Yeah," she said. "The twin spires from the paintings."

"We've got to be close."

No rattlesnake meat, but we each had a granola bar and a bottle of water for dinner. I banked the fire and found a place to curl up. I looked over and Claude was shaking.

"What if we don't get home?"

"Hey, you and I are both woodsmen," I said. I tried to smile to be reassuring. "This is our home. Enjoy the fresh air while you've got it. Tomorrow night, you'll be back sleeping in stale air-conditioned air."

"Think so?"

"Sure of it."

He was still shaking. Rue went over and put her arm around him, pulled his head onto her shoulder and stroked his hair.

"We'll be fine," she said. "Paul will take care of us."

"I've got to," I said. "Need to get you back to civilization so you can pay for my truck."

"Ain't paying for the truck," Claude said. "Her fault for shooting me the bird."

Rue's back stiffened and I thought she was going to put Claude to sleep with a rock up the side of his head. But I could see her make a conscious effort to relax and keep stroking his hair. "Shush," she said. "Don't say anything more. Just breathe in slowly. Let it out. Concentrate on your breathing. Breathe slow, count and let me know when you get to a hundred."

He was snoring before he had time to get to ten.

"Therapy?" I said.

"Jealous?"

"Yes."

"Good."

I napped a while, woke up sore from sleeping on the rock. Got up and stretched and decided to walk around to loosen up. I climbed up the slope, picking my steps in the dark. There was a big rock and I climbed up on it and sat there suspended among the stars and gathering clouds. Hanging in the pine-scented air a hundred yards over Rue I thought that if I was going to die, this was a beautiful place for it.

There was a crash of thunder and buckets of water poured down and washed away my serene vision. There was a flash of lightning and I thought I saw a silhouette of one of the tall, thin aliens from The Beacon mural. When the light faded, I stared but couldn't find him in the rain.

But off in the distance, there was a light winking on and off.

CHAPTER 47

The fire and I both were drenched by the time I got back to Rue and Claude. My hands were shaking with cold and excitement as I scraped together a few dry sticks and re-started the fire under the ledge. I took off my shirt and pants and huddled over the fire for warmth.

The sun was just coming up when Rue stirred and smiled at me.

"Finally got you almost naked, and we have a chaperone."

"Yeah." My teeth were still chattering.

"Seriously, are you trying to smoke yourself?"

"I got drenched in the night. Trying to warm up."

"Like to help."

"Dry wood would help."

She pulled away from Claude.

"Not what I had in mind, but I'll see what I can do."

She disappeared and came back with an armful. Piled it on the fire and went off again. By the time she was back, the fire was roaring and I was warm and mostly dry. She piled another load on.

"Better?" she said.

"Better. Few more minutes to let these clothes dry and we can head out."

She looked at the sunrise, oranges and purples behind the twin spires in the distance.

She nuzzled over and rubbed my arm. "Shame to leave. This

would be a beautiful place to stay."

"I saw a light in the woods last night."

She pulled back.

"So we may not die here?" she said.

"You never know."

"I'll wake up Sir Galahad."

"Let me put my pants on first."

We cleaned up and went up the trail, Rue bouncing ahead, Claude grumbling and falling behind. We got to the rock and I pointed in the direction of the light.

"I don't see any sign of people," said Rue.

"We're not there yet."

"Still, if people live around here, you'd expect to see something."

"Maybe. Remember what the bartender said about people up here not wanting to be found?"

"Yeah."

We climbed up to the top of a small rise.

"Looked like it came from about here," I said. "Let's spiral down from the top here and see if we find anything."

"A Waffle House would be nice," she said.

No Waffle House. Just a brush and a pile of rocks from an ancient rockslide.

Claude said, "Any more granola bars?"

"We ate the last food at breakfast."

"Water?" he said. "I drank mine."

"Sorry."

Rue said, "Paul, we need to think about giving up, trying to find that fire spotter tower, see if we can get a cell signal and get out of here."

"Yeah," I said. "Give up on this. Probably a good idea to stay alive."

"We'll come back."

"If the police let us. If we get out of here to begin with. Should have gone the other way. Probably be back in Jerome by now."

"Maybe."

I had been scanning the ground. Now I looked up at the top of the clump of trees at the top of the rise.

"Look," Rue said.

Rue was pointing at something metal among the trees.

"Satellite dish?" she said.

"Probably a solar cell."

We looked and saw a cable on the ground disappearing into the rocks. I stood up.

"There," I said.

A deep voice with a French accent came from the brush behind us. "What is your name?"

When I turned, there was no one there.

"I am Paul," I said.

From behind a tree, a tall, thin, dark-skinned teen-aged boy stepped out. Before I could say anything, an even taller and thinner woman stepped out of a cave in the rocks, with a small child by her side. She had no expression except for a kind of permanent sadness.

"We have been expecting you," she said.

CHAPTER 48

The woman turned and walked back into the cave, regal as a queen and with no doubt we would follow. I followed into a small opening in the rocks, past a canvas door that the woman held open, and into darkness. Once we were all inside, she languidly tied the canvas closed and flipped a switch. A small string of tiny white lights winked on like stars above our heads.

My eyes adjusted. I could see a small room with wooden cots along one wall and a small propane stove opposite. In the back, an artist's easel, paints and canvases were stacked up. The whole room smelled of cooking spices, hot peppers, cinnamon and . . . something else.

"Do you drink coffee?" she said to me.

"I'd rather drink coffee than breathe."

Her long sad face broke into a radiant smile.

"We have the best coffee on earth."

The boy stepped up to me. "I want to know where my father is."

His mother pulled him away and the sadness was back in her face.

"There will be time for that later. First our guests must be fed." She looked back at me and flashed the smile again. "And drink coffee."

She turned to a machine with intertwined copper tubes and filters.

"My name is Adela," she said with her back to me, "but, of

course, you know that."

She took a tin from a rock shelf and opened it. The room was filled with the richest coffee aroma I had ever smelled. She saw my look and smiled again.

"We brought this coffee with us from Leongo. In all modesty, it is the richest in the world."

"One smell convinced me."

She measured a serving into a small conical bowl on the top of the machine.

"I've never seen a coffee machine like that."

She took a pot off a tiny charcoal stove and slowly poured water onto the grounds, swirling it as she went. "You've never been to Leongo. This is how we brew our coffee there. It is a combination of a French press and a drip." The water bubbled and darkened and flowed through the tubes into the cup at the bottom. When it was full, she handed me the cup and bowed like it was an offering.

"And that," she said, "is why our coffee is the best on earth."

I took a sip, and it was. We both smiled.

We sat around a small table while she served us flat cakes and a spicy bean paste and the boy paced and glowered.

I pointed at the paints.

"Jean-Paul's paints," she said. "The woman has been teaching him how to paint. He wishes to be an artist here, and the organization that the woman belongs to—that you and the woman belong to—is helping him to become established. He was an art history professor, back home, but here he wishes to create."

"So you were professionals in Leongo?"

She laughed. "Does that surprise you? Did you expect us to run barefoot though the jungle with bones in our noses? Leongo was a civilized country, until the Man from God came."

"I have heard of the Man from God . . . but only a little.

From one of your countrymen, I'm sure . . . up in Portland. He too had . . ." I nodded toward the slash scars on her arm.

Her eyes dimmed in response. "Leongo is a small country, lost in the misfortunes of larger countries like the Sudan or Croatia."

She turned her arm so I could see the three slashes.

"The army of the Man from God comes in the night. The army is made up of children, stolen from their parents. The men in the army—if men is the right word for vermin like them—go through and mark the parents with three slashes. And then the families are left to sit and wait."

"My husband and I sat and held our children and cried, knowing what would come. It seemed like too long and too short a time, but soon the whole army returned, laughing and drunk and pulling my young daughter's clothes off and drinking my husband's wine. They were only boys themselves, but they put a machete in the hands of my son Jean-Paul, named after his father. Told him he must kill his parents, and become part of the army. When he hesitated, they tortured my daughter and told Jean-Paul that they would torture us all if he did not kill us. For most boys in Leongo, it is no choice at all.

"But my Jean-Paul is a young man, and not a boy. He swept the machete over my husband and suddenly the head of the man in charge fell, still laughing, at my feet. My husband grabbed the machete of the dead man, and together my husband and my son slaughtered the boys in our house and we ran.

"We ran knowing that running was futile. But one day, a man from your organization—your blessed organization—hid us in the back of a truck under crates of chickens and we drove and we drove until he stopped the truck and told us we were safe.

"They put us in the belly of a big green airplane. We flew for a very long time and landed in a darkened field with strange smells. They handed us papers and told us not to lose them, that these papers proved that we were now citizens of a new country. They asked us what kind of life we wanted. Men drove us here and told us to wait while things were arranged. One day the woman came to show my husband how to paint."

I interrupted. "Is she still here?"

"No. The woman has gone. She said a man—you—would come soon, and take us to a city to start our lives." Adela hesitated. "The woman said you were her husband once, before the man she is with now. No?"

I thought about my answer and Adela, tired of waiting, went on.

"I asked her once what was her name, and she said she had no name anymore. I said I would call her, 'Madame,' a title of honor usually reserved for married women. She smiled a sad smile and said, 'No, . . . Mademoiselle.' "

She paused.

"I think Mademoiselle must be a great woman."

I stood there with my stomach churning and didn't answer.

"Mama?" said Jean-Paul.

She nodded, slow and solemn.

"It is time," she said. She folded her hands and waited for me.

I looked at her a long time and didn't know what to say.

She put her hand on mine. "Just say it."

"Your husband—um—has been killed."

Jean-Paul spat out something short and ugly in French behind me, but Adela just nodded.

"So many times in Leongo. So close to death. So sure it was coming for us. Now, to die here."

"It was the art dealer," said Jean-Paul. "I will kill him."

Adela said, "Was it?"

"We don't know," I said. "It may have been a man who

worked for Crosswinds, the gallery owner. It may have been an accident."

She nodded gravely. "Jean-Paul took some of his paintings to this man, along with a letter from the woman. He was supposed to stay there and call you and tell you the woman wanted you here. You would come and then you and Jean-Paul would come back and move us into town.

"But Jean-Paul came back by himself. He said the man—Crosswinds—had taken his paintings and painted someone else's signature over his. Jean-Paul came back for one more painting to show people that he was the artist."

She looked down at her hands.

"I said it was a dangerous and foolish thing to do, but he said this was America and he would be OK."

We sat in silence for a few minutes, except for Jean-Paul cursing quietly in the corner.

"Adela," I said. "Do you know what was in the letter Jean-Paul took to Crosswinds from M—from the woman?"

"I have a copy."

CHAPTER 49

Adela brought a backpack over and opened it on the table. "Here are the papers they said we need to have to prove we belong here."

I looked at them. "I'm not an expert, but it looks like you're legal."

She handed me a checkbook. "The woman said this would be enough for us to get started."

I looked. "This should let you buy a house and cover you until you find a job. Any idea where this came from?"

"She said they have money, and they will get more if we need it."

I handed it back.

"Oh, here," she said. "Here is a copy of the letter she said to take to Mr. Crosswinds."

I took the sheet and looked at Rue. She nodded.

Mr. Crosswinds,
Please forgive me for not revealing my name in this letter. I am an art collector and expert who has been instrumental in discovering new talent. However, for my own reasons, I prefer to remain anonymous.

The artist who is presenting this letter is Mr. Jean-Paul Chrisafis, a new artist who has recently arrived in this country. I believe that his work will prove to be both

238

influential and popular. Specifically, I believe him to be the artistic inheritor of the new school recently founded by the late Marta Strauss-McClaron. I think his work will increase in both attention and value in the same pattern that the art world has recently seen in Ms. Strauss-McClaron's work.

Thank you for any consideration you can give Mr. Chrisafis. I believe your partnership with him will prove satisfying and profitable to both of you.

"So this is the letter your husband took to Crosswinds?"

She nodded.

"From the woman?"

She nodded.

I handed the letter to Rue. "This sounds like her. Trying to bully the world her way, well-intentioned but without a thought to the consequences. She thought everybody had something dirty to hide, so she appealed to his greed. Didn't know how right she was, at least about him. Crosswinds looked at this letter and saw an opportunity to forge the paintings."

Adela sat up straight. "My Jean-Paul would never go along with that."

"Sounds like he didn't. Maybe Crosswinds thought your husband was crooked and offered him a cut of the money. Maybe he thought no one would believe your husband did the paintings himself. In any case, something went wrong. We may never know what."

"We must go to the police," said Adela. "You have a truck here to move us to town?"

I looked at Claude. "We had a truck. Now we have feet."

"There is a man who lives in the valley," said Adela. "He will take us to town for money. My son will climb the fire tower on the hill. There, his cell phone will work. The man will come and get us."

"I want to go with your son to the tower."

Jean-Paul muttered the whole way about what he would do to the man who killed his father. I was silent with my own thoughts. Rue, bless her, managed to keep us from having to drag Claude along with us. We climbed the tower. Jean-Paul made his call, and I made mine.

"Ahlstrom," was the answer on the phone.

"This is Paul."

"Where the hell are you? If you're going to take off like that we're going to have to play rougher."

"I need you to play rough. Specifically, I need you to play rough with Crosswinds, owner of the gallery. I think he knows where the security guard Simon is. I need you and Owl to get to Crosswinds, find Simon, and bring him into town. Tell the chief I'm coming into town with some people he needs to meet. Tell him we'll see him at the Mom 'n Pop this afternoon."

"And if we bring them in, we'll get Marta and the money?"

"Probably not."

"Yeah, right. We're supposed to go get this guy, commit forty-seven crimes to get him to tell us what you want to know, and get nothing for it. I can't think of one reason to do this."

"Because you're still a cop," I said. "You'll always be a cop. And you'll always want to catch the perps."

CHAPTER 50

Claude and Rue, Adela and her daughter, were sitting on rocks by the cave when Jean-Paul and I got back. There were only two backpacks beside them.

"You travel light," I said.

Adela laughed, and it was a high tinkling laugh from someone who had learned to laugh at anything she could.

"This is a wealth of possessions for us," she said.

"No," I said, "we need one thing more."

I ducked past the canvas flap and came out with the coffee machine and a bag of beans. I handed the bag to Claude. He grumbled but agreed to carry it.

"You'll want this," I said told Adela. "Where you're going, the world is filled with instant coffee and everything is hurried. You'll want to have this. Remind yourself every morning of where you came from and why you're here."

Adela smiled down at me. Taller than me, elegant, unhurried, her arm flowed out at me and her hand stroked my cheek like she was petting a kitten.

"You are a man of kindness, Paul of America."

She turned and started down the hill in long, easy strides.

Rue said, "She is right, Paul of America."

"High praise, Rue of the Universe."

Claude walked with Adela and I hung back and watched them. Adela, graceful and calm, floating down the hill as if it were her home. Claude stumbling through a land that was his home, trying to keep up. Adela put out a hand and stopped Claude and we all caught up with them.

"There." She pointed at a rattlesnake coiled on the path ahead of us.

Claude picked up a stick.

"No," said Adela. "Respect his home."

The rattlesnake uncoiled and went on his way.

"I don't know how you live like this," said Claude. "No cars, no TV, nothing."

She laughed. "That is not the things that I miss."

Claude was silent. "I've never heard stories like you told."

Adela looked at him for a long time, smiled and put her hand on his cheek.

"It is hard to learn to respect someone different from yourself, no? Do you know why the Man of God is killing my people? What horrible difference we have that makes us monsters in his eyes?" She paused. "We are tall. He is short. So God told him to kill us."

She laughed like it was a wonderful joke and led us on down the path. When we got to the fire road, an impossibly old pickup truck, more rust than metal, was waiting. A shrunken white man with a mottled beard to his waist was leaning on it.

"Be careful stepping up here," he said, helping Adela into the bed. "If you step on those rusty places, you'll fall through and break my truck."

One side of the truck bed was rusted away completely. Rue and I sat with our backs to the cab. Adela and the others leaned against the one functioning side. Rue leaned past me.

"Adela," she said, "you might not want to mention Marta—the woman—to other people. Not by name. Maybe even change her description or something." She looked at me.

I thought.

"No. Let them think what they want." I laughed. "Ahlstrom

and Owl will just think it's a trick, anyway."

I pointed out over the edge at the twin spires in the distance.

"Your husband and my wife learned to paint alike. They took common things like that rock out there and made them something beautiful."

"Someday," Adela said, "I would like to see your wife's paintings."

"I'd like that."

"But you're wrong about that rock. It is not a common thing. It is beautiful. This country here is so beautiful. Leongo was beautiful in a very green way. This country is beautiful in a red and brown way. I wonder if I will ever fit in here. We have money to live on, but I wish to do something, to bring something to other people's lives. In Leongo, I was a doctor. Now, I do not think I could bear to look at another broken body. I wonder if I will ever find something small and clean and simple."

I looked at her. "You'll find something. Someday, you will see people smile from what you do."

Jean-Paul shifted.

"Someday," he said. "I will find a way to kill the man who killed my father. And then I will return to Leongo, and I will find ways to kill the soldiers there. And then I will kill the Man of God."

Rue reached across and patted Jean-Paul's hand.

"We are in a civilized country. Justice will find the man responsible for your father's death."

Jean-Paul pushed her hand away.

"And when will justice find my country?"

CHAPTER 51

I held the Mom 'n Pop door open for the others. The scene inside hadn't changed: aging militia on one side, Alice and the granola girls on the other, the chief and a few officers in the middle. They all turned and watched.

Adela stepped in beside me, sad-eyed, regal and quiet. Young Jean-Paul and the daughter joined her. The three of them stood silent and awkward, swaying like three out-of-place willows.

"Aliens," yelled one of the militia.

"Illegal aliens," said the man with the walker.

"No," I said. "Guests. Welcome guests." I took the papers to the chief. "Can you look at this and verify that the Chrisafises are here legally?"

He looked at the papers a minute, then turned to the militia.

"Looks like they're legal. You boys need to calm down." He turned back to me and waved one document.

"This the man who was the victim?"

I nodded.

"Weren't no victim," said the militia with the walker. "Was breaking in to steal from the gallery, from all of us Americans. Deserved what he got. Proves he was one of them, no matter what them papers say. That's what these people do, break in and just take, take, take."

He glared at Adela. She tried a calm smile but it wasn't returned. Jean-Paul took a step toward the militia and they cringed at the boy who was already a head taller than any of them. Adela put her hand on Jean-Paul's forearm and he stopped.

Rue stepped into the middle of the room.

"He wasn't taking, he was giving. He didn't break in to steal. He broke in to add his own painting to the gallery. He was making a contribution. Wanted to be one of you."

Chief Collins looked at me.

"It's true," I said. "If you look in the gallery, you'll find one painting with the signature 'Jean-Paul Chrisafis.' The other paintings were done by Chrisafis, too. Crosswinds painted over the signature to try to up the price. We can prove it."

The militiamen were silent, but Alice was not.

"So you've just proven that this pseudo-Nazi guard Simon shot an innocent man, shot him out on the sidewalk, another example of police brutality?"

"We don't know that," I said. "I think I've got an answer coming on that." I hesitated. "Maybe."

"Then we'll wait," said the chief.

We all shuffled around for a couple of minutes and nobody said anything. I kept looking at the door that never opened. The chief kept looking at me. I felt like I needed to do something

"While we're waiting, Alice," I said. "How about some coffee?"

"You know I won't serve you our coffee. Go to the coffee shop in town for fancy Portland coffee."

I said, "How about something better than coffee house coffee?"

Rue was ahead of me. She snatched up the Leongolian coffee maker and set it up on a corner table.

I said, "Ms. Chrisafis here makes a very exotic coffee with beans that are found only in her former country on Leongo, with her own technique. Like nothing you've ever tasted."

Adela was standing silent, a little proud and a little shy.

"May she make you a cup?" Rue said to Alice.

"Our coffee's plenty good," Alice said. She hesitated and glared at Henry. "But unlike some people here, I believe in being neighborly and giving other people a chance."

Alice pranced over and took Adela's hand and gave her a big smile. "I would just love to try some of your coffee."

They walked over to the table and went to work together.

Alice fussed over her shoulder to Henry. "See, Henry, we don't have to go copying all the out-of-towners. We've got our own fancy coffee, right here from a local."

Adela smiled bigger.

Henry said, "Maybe."

Adela and Alice chattered as they ground the beans and brewed the coffee, Adela's smoky French accent and Alice's Arizona twang blending like colors in a painting.

Adela took the first cup and held it out to Alice. The room was filling with a dark, smoky warmth that called to us all.

Alice shook her head. "Let that old man try it, see if we've got something good enough to impress him. He likes it, we'll make a cup for everybody."

Every head turned to Henry, praying, I thought, that he'd give the right answer. Alice took the cup in both her hands like a chalice and offered it to Henry. Henry took a long sip, and handed Adela back an even warmer smile.

"This is the best," he said, "on earth."

CHAPTER 52

The militia and the granola girls were lining up for Adela's coffee, starting to mingle together, when Ahlstrom and Owl came in, pushing Crosswinds ahead of them. Crosswinds had a black eye and a bloody scalp and was holding one arm. The chief looked up at Crosswinds without emotion and took a long sip of his own coffee.

"What happened to you?" he finally said.

"They beat me, Chief. They—"

"He fell down," said Owl interrupting the battered gallery owner.

"A lot," said Ahlstrom.

Crosswinds stepped away from them and got brave.

"Like hell! Chief. I want to file charges . . ."

"You fell down," said the chief. "Do you need to go outside with these gentlemen and get your story straight?"

Crosswinds hesitated. "No."

The chief looked fiercely at Crosswinds. "I hear that you've been changing signatures on paintings."

Crosswinds hesitated. "So what, they're my paintings."

"Could be fraud," said the chief. "Could be worse."

"Not if I haven't tried to sell them yet."

"Could be right. Maybe there's nothing I can charge you with. We'll see."

The chief looked at Ahlstrom. "You got anything else?"

"Yeah. Mr. Crosswinds here graciously volunteered to take us to a hunting cabin of his. We found someone there."

Ahlstrom stepped aside and Simon walked in. He lit up when he saw the chief.

"Chief, Mr. Crosswinds wouldn't let me go. He took the keys to my truck and wouldn't let me go. I told him I had to come tell you what happened, but he wouldn't let me go."

"Suppose you tell me now."

"I took the job with Mr. Crosswinds like you told me to and I was protecting the store every night and nothing got stolen. Then the last night there Mr. Crosswinds give me a gun, told me that a bad man was coming, a tall, black man, and that I would need to have a gun because the bad man was killing people and he would kill me. So when I heard a noise that night, I went out into the front room and the bad man was standing there with a hammer in his hand fixing to kill me."

The chief nodded. "Or maybe he had the hammer from hanging a painting."

"I don't know. Maybe. But he was going to kill me. Mr. Crosswinds told me he was going to kill me and I had to kill him first."

"What then?"

"I shot him, then I called Mr. Crosswinds like he told me to. When he got there, I told him we had to call you. He said, 'Like hell we do,' and started to drag the dead man out to his car to put him in his trunk. He had him out on the sidewalk when I made him bring the body back, told him you would want the body just where it was. But it left blood all over the place. Mr. Crosswinds told me to get in my truck and follow him out to his cabin, that you were there waiting for us. When we got there, he took my keys and told me you'd be there soon. But you never came."

"I'm sorry I wasn't there for you, Simon," said the chief. "Sorry I let you get mixed up with a bad man." He looked at

Crosswinds. "A real bad man."

Alice came over and sat Simon at a table by the chief.

"Why don't you let me bring you some breakfast, son, while you and the chief sort this out? I think you've been mistreated." She looked back at the granola girls. "Maybe by all of us."

The police were collecting statements. The Meteor citizens—no longer militia and granola girls, just neighbors—were having coffee and talking with the Chrisafises. I heard Henry trying to recruit Jean-Paul for the high school basketball team, Jean-Paul asking if basketball was anything like soccer. Changes were clearly coming for all of them.

I sat down across from Ahlstrom and Owl. They stood up, came around so I was boxed in between the two of them. Rue came over and stood opposite us, not sitting, just watching and ready.

"We did our job," said Owl. "Now you owe us."

"What do I owe you?"

"Five million dollars," said Owl.

"Marta," said Ahlstrom.

"I've got neither."

"Then you've got us. You might fall down some like Crosswinds did."

I nodded. "No problem. You guys want to stick with me, fine. But I don't want to fall down like Crosswinds."

I turned over and put my finger in Ahlstrom's face.

"You're getting paid expenses by the insurance company, right?"

"Yeah."

"So you've got a paid vacation, go anywhere you like, as long as I'm there."

Ahlstrom didn't say anything.

"But know this: the minute I call up the insurance company

and formally relinquish claim to that policy, they will cut you off and the ride will stop."

I paused and let that sink in.

"So hang around, investigate, do what you do. But no rough stuff, or you can go back to Portland and live off your pension."

Owl said, "Fair deal, long as you give me five million dollars."

I turned to him. "You see yourself as some sort of white knight, reclaiming money for your people?"

He shrugged. "Red knight, maybe, according to you racists. But yeah, on my good days, I'm proud of what I do."

"But you know that most of that five million will never make it to your people."

He didn't say anything but all of us knew the answer.

"So here's the deal. Larry and I have a warehouse full of Marta's paintings back in Portland. I don't need the money. As long as I stay healthy, the money from those paintings goes to you, for you to distribute to the tribe. No middlemen, no tribal council, no money for you. Deal?"

He smiled and nodded.

"Anything happens to me," I said, "and we all lose."

Ahlstrom leaned and put his arm around my back to Owl's, holding us both.

"Buddies," he said.

"No," said Owl and I together.

CHAPTER 53

Rue and I slipped out of the Mom 'n Pop alone, walking home. Her hand was in mine and the sunshine never felt better.

"So it's all fixed now?" she said.

I made a face. "Don't you start. I'm not a fixer."

"Sure you are. You're a fixer. Got to make everything right. Just can't help yourself. It's not a bad thing."

"I'm a shambling lazy river bum who just wants to drift where the current goes."

"So you think. Ready to go back to the condo, get a shower, and see where the current goes?"

"I'd like to, but I've got one more thing to do. Something I can't fix. Think you can get us into the art gallery?"

She studied my face.

"Sure," she said. "I have an errand to run this afternoon anyway." She grinned. "Something I can't tell you about."

I stood in the gallery alone after Rue left. There was still blood on the floor and paintings on the wall that Marta had taught someone to paint. I looked back and forth, not focusing on them, until I finally forced myself to look at the one painting I had come to see.

The background scene in the top left was the same twin spire that showed up in so many of the paintings. But when I had looked at the painting on Rue's phone, I thought something was different, something I couldn't quite make out.

I was right.

At the base of the spires was a stream that didn't exist in any of the other paintings and didn't exist with the real spires. I bent close and saw a man in a boat paddling along the stream. On the shore was a black-haired woman with her head in her arms, miserable. I looked at it for a long time, wondering how much of what I saw was in the painting, and how much was in my interpretation. But I knew who the man and woman were, and who had painted this picture.

I moved on to the next detail. Again, the main scene was another Arizona landscape. But at the base this time, the man in the boat was gone. The black-haired woman had turned into a superhero with a sword, battling a horrible monster while smaller people cowered behind her. Each scene after that was another rescue. Different people, different settings. The black-haired woman pulled a man from a cliff. The black-haired woman fought gunmen in a city with just her sword.

Finally, I came to a scene with four impossibly tall, thin black figures. Behind them stood four white figures holding hands: a man I didn't recognize, the black-haired woman, a tall, sandy-haired man like me, and another woman holding his hand. I stood staring at if for a long time wondering what it meant. Wondering how the sandy-haired man made it into the picture.

There was one last scene that made no sense: just a small bar in a strip mall by a creek in front of a red rock. There was lettering on the bar, but I couldn't read it.

I tore into Crosswinds' office, looking for a magnifying glass. Couldn't find one until I noticed that his desk lamp was one of the old style with a round magnifying glass set inside a circular bulb. I ripped the lamp off the desk and carried it back to the painting.

Squinted at the painting until I could read, "Dry Creek Grill." Looked in the phone book and found the address and ran out the door.

CHAPTER 54

I was in the gallery parking lot before I stopped running. Remembered that I had no truck, and Meteor had no public transit.

I stopped, lost. In my world, I had always leaned on The Beast, on the reliability of familiar things. Now the ten-minute drive would take what suddenly seemed like forever. I felt lost.

Then I thought of Rue's world and what she would do. I stepped to the road and put my thumb out. It felt unnatural, even alien, but I did it.

Ten minutes later, I stood alone in the parking lot of a strip mall, waving goodbye to a rusty minivan of Buddhist monks singing Led Zeppelin songs and wishing me good fortune as they drove away. There was a dentist's office and a hiking store. And the last small suite had the sign, "Dry Creek Grill" over it.

I opened the door into a dark room, hard-core country music growling from the jukebox. Three young men in a corner were trying to get the attention of a tall, beautiful, black-haired woman staring into the space over their heads. Marta. In an instant, I remembered how much that aloofness had once attracted me. She saw me and stared for a minute without smiling.

"I quit," she said to the man at the register.

"What you mean, you quit?"

She walked past him toward the door with no recognition for him or me.

"Won't be back. Burn my check for all I care."

She had her cell out as she hit the door. "Now," she said into it and snapped it shut.

She sat down on a bench under an Alligator Juniper in front of the stores and patted a place for me. I sat down, a foot away from her.

She scooted over to me, hip to hip. Reached up and stroked my cheek. Her touch was strong and hot, not tender. I remembered how much I missed the fire that she brought to even little things.

She put her hand on my cheek and smiled.

"I knew you'd come to me."

I had something to say but she dropped her hand to my thigh and kissed me. I felt the same intense aura, the feeling that Marta held something wonderful beyond imagining.

She whispered in my ear. "Too much water under the bridge between us for you to walk away, to mangle the old saying."

She laughed, low and sexy, but it didn't matter.

I pulled back.

"You think that's funny?" I said. "You disappear; hurt everybody who ever cared about you, and now it's just a stupid joke? I used to think I just couldn't understand you because you felt and thought things more deeply than me. Now it all seems like a stupid cruel joke."

She pulled back, too, and stuck a finger in my face. "You listen to me. I did what I did for both of us. I did it for the whole damned world. We were living little lives, you paddling down little rivers and me creating paintings too big for little people to comprehend while the world burned around us. The organization I'm with now finds people who need help, brings them here and gives them new lives. You're going to join us. You're too much of a Boy Scout to turn down that kind of an opportunity to help people."

She leaned back into me, tracing circles on my chest with her finger.

"Besides," she said, "you really do miss me, whether you know it or not."

Her hand moved back to my thigh, higher now.

I said, "Your organization also robs people. Leaves other people on the hook."

She put her head on my chest and purred into me.

"What we do takes money, honey. Besides, I covered for you."

I started to tell her how well that had worked, but I doubted if she would hear me.

"I even made a place for you here," she went on. "You had a try-out. Jean-Paul was supposed to call you for help getting settled, tell you that I needed you. We wanted someone who couldn't be traced to the organization. You were perfect. It got more complicated, but you did a good job, fixed things like I told them you would. Now the organization wants you."

She moved her hand up to my stomach, missing nothing on the way. "And I want you."

I pushed her hand away.

I stood up. "Marta, I'm done with lying to myself about you. About us. I've been papering over problems and hiding in old movies and the past when I should have been building my own life."

She waved her hand. "That's so bourgeoisie. We were built for more."

It hit me as soon as she said it: she was right. She was built for something more than what we ever had together.

And I realized that I, too, was built for something more than what I had been living. Suddenly, the pain that had driven me for six months was gone and I knew what I wanted. I started to say something but she interrupted.

"Besides," she said, "you've got to keep my secret. My paintings and the work that I do—both of them will get hurt if people find out I'm alive."

I thought about it. "I'll keep your secret. And I'll be there if you need help. I owe that much to the good times. I forgive you, now, for all the bad things. Part of me will always admire the crazy girl who lives in a big way, even if she leaves a path of destruction in her wake. But I want something real now for myself. My life isn't yours, anymore."

She smiled a little cat-smile and said, "We'll see."

A black SUV pulled up. The blond driver looked at Marta and tapped his wrist. She kissed me again, the memories flooding back. When she pulled away, she said, "You still want me."

I pointed at the driver. "What's he to you? In this brave new world you want for us, how would he fit into things?"

Marta laughed. "Rolf? Don't tell me you haven't found a little something on the side. You can have us both."

She stood up. "But you have to decide. Now."

I kissed her on the forehead.

"I don't want you both." I stepped away from her. After months of not being able to turn loose, it was easier now than I ever expected. "I want the whole universe."

CHAPTER 55

I sat on the bench and watched the SUV pull away. Stood up, took two steps walking and then broke into a run. Didn't stop running until finally—near exhaustion—I burst into the door of the condo. Rue was sitting on the floor, naked and in a lotus position, incense curling around her head. She smiled and wrinkled her nose. After I had spent a lifetime admiring nature's beauty, Rue, naked and natural, here and now, was the most beautiful thing I had ever seen.

"You need a shower."

"I need more than that." I bounded up the stairs. Stopped at the top. "I'll get a shower, quick. You get some hiking clothes on."

"Really? Really? This makes you think of hiking?" She waved her hand over her body.

"Trust me."

When I came out, she was dressed and grumbling.

"The whole universe shouting one simple idea in your ear, and you can't hear a word of it."

"Please trust me just a few minutes more."

We walked up the hill to the base of Wave Rock. Sat down on that same hidden ledge from our first night in Meteor.

I said, "I want our first time of . . . therapy to be beautiful."

I unbuttoned her top button and she smiled.

"I want us to make our own beauty," I said. "I want us to use the colors of your universe—our universe—to make our own paintings." I motioned to the crimson western sky, orange ball just now setting on the horizon.

"Wait," she said when we were naked and the colors of the sky were starting to flow over her. "I want to try something I've never done before. Have you ever tried tantric sex?"

"Never heard of it."

"OK, trust me."

She arranged me into a cross-legged sitting position.

"Remember that first night at your house, when I was trying to loosen you up?"

"Oh yeah."

She sat in my lap and wrapped her arms and legs around me.

"This is kind of like that, only a little . . ." she settled into me in one last move ". . . different."

"Different," I said.

She whispered, "The idea is to sit very still, make it last a long time."

We sat for a minute before she said, "Stop that. You're moving."

"No," I said. "You're moving."

"No." Her voice got husky. "Stop that."

"You stop," I said.

Our breathing quickened and blended into one.

"Don't stop," she said.

Later, when we were still sitting wrapped together in the gathering dusk, I said, "That's some therapy. Is it always like that?"

Her head was nuzzled into my shoulder.

"Don't know," she said. "That's my first time doing this as therapy. My first anything since the old boyfriend."

We sat and listened to the night noises coming up.

"But so you know," she said. "This is just therapy."

"Therapy," I said.

"Therapy," she whispered into my shoulder.

But the stars were coming out, and they had never been brighter.

CHAPTER 56

I knew she would be there before my eyes even opened, before I felt the small flowing warmth of her breath rocking my bed, before I knew anything from my senses. I knew, and I thanked the universe for the knowing. I rolled over and there she was.

I put my arm around her, felt the power of the moment when my skin touched hers, and ran my hand down her and felt the sense of contact spread across her throat, breasts, stomach, thighs.

She moaned and shivered.

"I knew," she said. "I knew this moment would come."

She held my arm and rolled over within it.

"I knew," she said, "when I finally drifted off to sleep last night that this moment would come, the first morning touch. I almost didn't go to sleep."

I looked into her face and saw a million things I had never seen before. I started to say one thing, shut my mouth and started to say something else.

"Shhh." She put one finger on my lips and I kissed it. She rolled over on me and said it all.

We sat on the bed, later, with our suitcases packed.

"Sure you won't fly back with me?" I said. "Glad to pay for the ticket." I smiled. "I think I'd get my money's worth."

She smiled back. "You would. But I don't fly, and I don't let anybody pay for anything. Ever. I'll—never mind, I've got a way. I'll see you later." She picked up her backpack. "Besides, I've got a surprise for you downstairs." She hoisted the pack on one shoulder and I grabbed her hand.

"Look," I said. "I just want to be clear. As wonderful as this is, I've still got things to work out. I'm just not someone who can walk away from things easily."

She set the pack down and took my face in her hands.

"You love us both, and that's a big part of why I love you. You're the man who always seems to have enough for everybody."

We stayed there a long time locking eyes. She broke and dropped her hands.

"Besides, this is therapy."

She picked the pack up and walked to the door.

"Oh, forgot to tell you. I restarted your six month clock last night. Seemed fairer to count from then."

"Fairer."

"More therapeutic. See you downstairs."

Then she was gone and I was looking out the window and wondering what was out there for me. Rue's scent and warmth still hung in the room like a ghost. Somewhere outside the window, Marta was moving on with a life that could still intersect with mine at any time.

I had lived most of my life in the Pacific Northwest: cold, rainy but beautiful. Now I sat in a warm land the color of Rue's sunburned skin, always warm, always glowing. I wondered what else was out there.

I hoisted my pack and walked out the door, head down, feeling sorry for myself because I was about to fly and leave Rue and the earth. I opened the front door and stepped out into the world.

I looked up and Rue was sitting on the hood of a sky-blue 1960 Corvette with her red-brown legs crossed over the fender.

"Like it?" she said.

"I like the legs," I said. "Don't like what the owner's going to do when he catches you using his classic car for a couch."

She held up a set of keys and jingled them. "Mine."

"You? With a gas-guzzling, old-fashioned, impractical . . ."

". . . gorgeous, open-to-the-universe classic connection to the past and the future," she said. "The universe told me to buy it. The man at the lot said it was the original car from an old TV show."

"Route 66. Could be. Same year. Same color as the first year."

I looked at her.

"Better than hitching," I said. "But you have to baby her. These things are a joy, but they need a lot of care."

She took the backpack off my shoulder and strapped it on the luggage rack on the back.

"Good thing I know a fixer," she said.

I stood in the warm sunshine and ran my hand along the door.

"Compared to The Beast I've ridden in all my life, it almost seems fragile."

"It's got a strong engine."

She vaulted over the door and into the driver's seat with one smooth motion.

I thought about trying the same thing. Had an image of myself crashing into the windshield, smashing the radio and spending the day in the emergency room. I opened the door and sat down.

"Are we going straight home?" I said.

"We'll see," she said.

She backed out next to Ahlstrom and Owl, leaning against each other by their car. Ahlstrom held up his hand in what could have been a wave or the old TV Indian "how" sign. I thought about ignoring him but it seemed rude so I waved back.

"Keep up," I yelled.

Rue revved the engine, looked at the road to our left and to our right and said, "OK. You decide."

I said, "Follow the Universe?"

Rue smiled with the warmth and promise of a million suns.

I stretched my hand and grabbed the sky and let it fall all the way into Rue's lap.

Rue turned her smile toward the strange red landscape, popped the clutch and slammed us forever onto the open road.

ABOUT THE AUTHOR

Michael Guillebeau is the author of *Josh Whoever,* which was named a Mystery Debut of the Month by *Library Journal* and was a finalist for the Silver Falchion Award for Best First Novel: Literary Suspense. He has published over twenty short stories, including three in *Ellery Queen's Mystery Magazine. A Study in Detail* is based on a story of the same name published in the May 2011 issue of *EQMM.* Mike splits his time between Huntsville, Alabama and Panama City Beach, Florida. Mike is a member of MWA and Sisters in Crime.